Mountain
of Justice

Dark Secrets of a Serial Killer

A Novel by Bert Whitfield

Prologue

A small-town police homicide detective discovers that he has become the target of a homicidal maniac. Over the past ten years, this person has killed people all up and down the East Coast of the United States. In all the murder cases, the real perpetrator orchestrated a way to pin the blame on other people. The innocent people would end up in prison for life or on death row, while the deranged psychopath roamed free to continue his murderous killing spree. The real killer was a brilliant man with an IQ over two hundred. The killer is exceedingly dangerous and diabolical. He is always two to three steps in front of law enforcement and the unsuspecting victims. This shrewd manipulator calculates every move just as a professional chess player would do to win the game. In the end, realism sets in and fate falls heavy, but will justice prevail?

Chapter one

1:06 PM, Tuesday, August 3rd, 2007:

It's a hot day in Wilmington, NC when Tate Logan's cell phone unexpectedly starts to ring. He has just finished eating a tuna sandwich, with lettuce and tomato, a little mayo and a lot of hot sauce. Tate is a homicide detective with the Wilmington Police. Today is a vacation day that Tate has been looking forward to for a long time. As Tate looks at his phone, he can see that the number on caller ID is that of the Detective Division.

"Man… they know I'm on vacation!"
After several rings, Tate reluctantly answers.

"You know I am off today!"
It's his Captain, Brad Carter.

"Tate… I know you are off today. I hate to call you especially today, but I also know that you would want to know about this. It's one of your old friends. Tate, someone has killed Tony Johnson." Tate is quiet, not a sound for several seconds. Thoughts were running through Tate's head, as he slowly said;

"I just talked to him yesterday. We talked about going back to the mountains to do some fishing. This can't be... there's no way."

This was extremely upsetting and completely unexpected for Tate. Tate and Tony had been friends from the time they started high school. After graduating from school, they joined the Army, completed Basic Training and served as Military Police together. After serving in the military, Tony ran the family business, a little hardware store at the edge of town. Tate went into law enforcement and worked his way up to a police homicide investigator. They both had enjoyed the last thirty years doing what they loved. This would be a very difficult case for Tate, but Tate was the best detective on the force. As a matter of fact, he was the best in the state. This would be the most challenging and difficult case of Tate's entire career.

"Tate… Tate are you there?"

"Yes, Brad, I'm still on the phone. I just don't know how I am going to handle this. I just might be too close."

"Well, Tate we need you to get whoever did this. A Crime Scene Investigation Unit is in route now, and if you hurry you can get there about the same time they do. It happened at his hardware store."

"Okay Brad, I'll get there as soon as possible. Oh, by the way, has anyone notified the next of kin about Tony? If not, his sister is about the only one around here that's related to him. I'll stop by and give her notification if you think that's okay."

"That will be alright Tate, just make a note of it for your file." Captain Brad Carter, an African American male about fifty-five years old, had over thirty years of service with the Wilmington Police Department. He is a very respected leader in the Department and the community. Like a lot of the older officers, he is overweight and out of shape and can be very grumpy at times. He also has a reputation for looking after the officers.

When Tate hung up, he started to gather his material and his thoughts. *Who? And why? Tony had no enemies and everyone that knew him really liked him.* After a few minutes, Tate is on the way, with his mind racing. He knew he would be up to the challenge, but he had no idea what was in store for the next few weeks.

Tate grew up along the coast of NC, spending time on the water and loving to fish. For his age, he had maintained a good physique and was bronzed from the sun. He was tall, lanky and liked to smoke a cigar on occasion. His stature was intimidating to some, and his eyes were like steel. Those eyes seemed as if they could see right through you. He, like a lot of Police Detectives, was divorced and lived alone. He did, however, date different ladies on occasions, but Tate was not ready to marry at this point. Maybe someday, but not for now. His true love is, 'homicide investigations.' Sure, earlier in his life he had been married, but as hard as he tried the marriage still fell apart. Tate had no kids and most of his family had either died or lived out of state. Tate's experience spoke for itself, but he always had a sixth sense for quickly sizing up people. He had a way of acting very humble, which relaxed his suspects and caused them to think he might not be too smart. This inaccurate assumption usually ended up being a grave mistake, made by the suspect.

Tony was almost the exact opposite of Tate. He was short and stocky, and known as a fast-talking Italian from Long Island, New York. He came to America when he was only nine years old and quickly learned to speak English. His father changed their names from Russo to Johnson, shortly after they arrived, assuming it would make them all fit in better. Tony never liked it but with time, he accepted it. The family moved from Long Island to Wilmington when Tony started high school. He was aggressive and at times, somewhat loud and obnoxious. His dark hair was beginning to gray on the sides and his skin was smooth as silk. Tony had a sharp Italian accent and was sly as a fox. Once people got to know Tony, they soon liked him a lot. He had great stories to tell and was loyal to his friends. He, too, had been divorced for several years and had no children.

On the way to the store, Tate stopped by Tony's sister's house. Maria lived just a few blocks from the store. She and her husband were happily retired. As Tate drove up, he could see them both working in their garden next to the house. As Tate parked and got out, the two started to walk toward him. Maria and Al were both a little hot and sweaty. Maria wiped her face with her apron and Al wiped his hands with a handkerchief from his back pocket. Tate stopped at the edge of the garden and spoke;

"That's a very nice garden…looks like you and Al have really been working hard." This was hard for Tate. He dropped his head as the two stepped up to him. They could tell that something was not right.

"Tate, what's wrong? Are you okay?" Maria asked.

"Maria…I have some very bad news…" Then Tate thoughtfully and compassionately gave her the devastating news. She was very upset, but Al and Tate were there to comfort her.

"Tate…Who and why…? Tony loved everyone. Was it a robbery that went bad?" Maria asked.

"Maria, I don't know what happened. All I know is…Captain Carter called me just a few minutes ago and asked me to take the case. I was on vacation today and this hit me like a bolt from the blue. But I am going to do everything I can to find out what happened. I am also going to bring the person that did this to Tony in, and see justice carried out..."

"Oh Tate, please get whoever did this." Maria said as the tears ran down her face.

"If you and Al need anything, anything at all, please call me."
As Tate left, Tony's sister had a dazed and solemn expression on her face. She was filled with confusion. But there was nothing Tate could do or say to help her. Death notifications are usually done by law enforcement, especially in homicide cases. And, Tate was no stranger to giving the bad

news to unsuspecting family members, but it's a lot harder when it's someone that's close to you.

Now, while on the way to the hardware store, his mind flashed back to when he was just fifteen years old. It is his first day in the ninth grade at the new high school. He is a nervous, tall, skinny, and clumsy kid and he is late for his first class. He is headed down the hall while trying to read directions on a note that he is holding in front of him. There are several other kids in the busy hallway. Suddenly he and another student run into each other and when they collide, they, along with their books, hit the floor. The new kid just happens to be Tony Johnson.

"Watch where you go! You stupid, skinny fool!" Tony yells out, with his thick Italian accent.

"I'm sorry dude…I didn't see you." Tate said as the two get up and begin collecting their books and papers.

Tony was as mad as he could be. Seeing what was going on, one of Tate's friends came over and started to take up for him.

"Look Dude! Who do you think you are?! We'll kick your behind New Guy! You better watch it!"

"So, you wanna fight?! You think you wanna fight with me? I fight you any time, any place! You name!" Tony said, with his strong Italian accent.

"No! No man! It was my fault. I ran into you, I'm sorry!" Tate said, as a teacher was approaching, and they all were headed on to their classes, as fast as possible. Tony and Tate ended up in the same class that day and neither said a single word to each other. They also had the same lunch break, and as Tate's headed through the line getting his food, he spots Tony. He's sitting over at a table all alone with his brown paper bag. Tony brought his lunch, and no one wants to sit with the 'new guy.' Tate walked over to some of his friends and sat down to eat. While sitting there with his buddies, he began feeling bad for the new guy. He did not like what the other kids were saying about him either. So, after a few minutes, he got up and walked over to Tony's table.

"Hey man...I'm sorry about running into you earlier. Can I sit down and have lunch with you?"

"Whatever...I no care what you do...Just, no bother me, I like, to be alone."
Tate tried to make small talk with Tony, but he was not getting anywhere. Tony just didn't want to talk to Tate. Now, Tate said in frustration;

"Look Dude! I just want to be a friend! And if you can't get that in your thick head then I'll just leave you the heck alone!"

"Okay! Okay! I am sorry. I act like a jerk, but I don't need no babysitter!"

"And I don't want to be a babysitter either!"
At this point the tension in the air thinned out a bit and the two began to talk. Tate told Tony all about himself and Tony did the same. They were on their way to becoming friends. The one thing that Tate will never forget about Tony, was what he told him that first day in the lunchroom.

"If I like you...You KNOW...If I NO like you...You KNOW..."

As they became closer and time went by, the day came that they had to fight off an attack from a couple of the school bullies. Much to Tate's surprise, Tony's fighting skills were quite impressive. Tony was beating the pure living-hell out of both bullies, while Tate ended up just looking on in disbelief. From that day on, no one ever messed with Tate or Tony. Rumors started to run wild about Tony. This tough guy was hooked up with the Mafia and he had all kind of connections. Tate and Tony thought it was so funny. Who had ever seen anyone in the Mafia with a Johnson name? But one thing was for sure, they were not about to tell anyone anything different. They just would not make any comments about it at all. By doing that, it just made it look, as if there was a connection with the Mafia for sure.

All through high school the two stuck together. They double dated and played all kind of sports. Tony was good at soccer, while Tate was good at basketball, but neither were good enough to play at the college level. So, after they graduated the two joined the Army, and during their four years of service they really had some interesting encounters. They both were a couple of cutups to say the least. But they somehow managed to stay out of any trouble that would get them discharged.

Also, while in the Army, they both met their future wives and married. Tony was Tate's best man and Tate was Tony's best man. Tony married a sharp looking blonde from Manhattan, New York. Her name was Mary Ann or as Tony would call her 'Marr.' They had a somewhat up and down relationship, but everyone knew that they loved each other very much. And, Marr was very good to Tony, and likewise. When Tony and Tate were honorably discharged from the Army, they moved back to Wilmington. Mary Ann could not adjust to the southern lifestyle and left Tony about a year later. She moved back to Manhattan and Tony never heard from her again. Tate married Susan, a red head with a fiery temper. But, after ten years, she left him because she said he was constantly argumentative and impossible to please. This was not true as she was the one that always loved to argue. Tate just sat and smiled, and that smile was what drove her over the edge. Sure, she tried to say that it was his detective work that kept him away all the time, but she really was never happy with Tate.

Chapter two

1:39 PM:

Tate pulls into the parking lot at 4905 Old
Bridge Road, Johnson's Hardware Store,
Wilmington NC. He could see that the CSI
(Crime Scene Investigation) team has already
arrived. There are several vehicles parked
near the lot and the crime scene is draped
with yellow crime-scene tape. Three police
cars are parked in the area and two police
officers are controlling the scene. Tate can
see Tony's car parked near the side door of
the shop. Tate parked his unmarked Crown
Vic, got out of his car, grabbed his briefcase
and walked over to one of the police officers.
The officer spotted Tate as he walked up.
Tate asked,

"Who discovered the crime and are they
still here?"

"Sir, it was a customer. A man named Sam
Curran came in and found Tony. He is
standing over by the front door near the

parking lot."

"Thanks, I'll go over and take a statement from him."

As Tate walked toward the building his eyes were scanning everything and everyone. He was looking for anything out of place or suspicious. On the way to the witness, he stopped by Tony's car. On the front seat of the 1969 Ford Gran Torino was the morning edition newspaper, folded next to an empty McDonald's coffee cup and a receipt from McDonald's. The window to the driver's side was open. While standing there, Tate sees another police officer standing near the witness. Tate headed toward the police officer. As he approached, he asked the police officer to safeguard the material in Tony's car. Afterwards, he identified himself to the witness.

"Hello Sir, my name is Detective Tate Logan with the Wilmington Police Department and I will be investigating this incident. What can you tell me about this?"

"Sir, my name is Samuel, J. Curran, 102 North Main St., Wilmington. I needed some half inch screws for a small job I was working on at my house, so I came down to the store. When I got here the front door was shut and the 'closed' sign was in the window."

"What time did you get here?" Tate asked.

"It was around 12:45 p.m. and right off, I thought this was out of the ordinary, because the store is never closed for lunch."

"So, what happened next?"

"Well, I looked in through the window to see if I could see anyone. At first, I had a hard time seeing anything due to the glare from the bright sun. But when I got close to the window, I saw Tony, or who I thought was Tony, laying on the floor over near the counter."

"Did you see anyone else inside the store?"

"No."

"What did you do then?"

"Heck! I called 911 and gave the information to the dispatcher. Within a few minutes, I could hear the police coming... and man were they coming."

"Did you see anyone or anything that

looked suspicious?"

"No... I did not see anything, or anyone."

"Okay, what else happened?"

"The first officer come up and I told him what I had seen. The police officer turned the doorknob and the door opened. He told me to stay right where I was. He then walked in and checked the store. He went all around inside the store with his weapon drawn. When the second officer arrived, she ran in with her weapon drawn. The two continued to search for anyone else that might have been inside, but then they yelled, all clear! The next thing I knew, CSI arrived and now, you."

"Okay Sir, I may need to ask you a few more questions later, but for now you can go."

Now, Tate walked inside the store and over to his friend's body. Tony was covered with blood, lying face down with the back of his head smashed in by a three-foot-long crowbar. Someone had really done him in and in a bad way. His wallet was in his right back pocket. As Tate looked around the store, it appeared that everything was intact, nothing seemed to be missing. It looked just like it always looked. He was often in the store to see his old friend, so Tate knew the store very well. The cash register was closed and appeared to have been undisturbed. The CSI were doing their jobs, taking photos and fingerprints and all other stuff that they do. CSI Officer Danny Smith was getting some good prints from the crowbar.

"We got this one Tate. We've got some really good stuff here." Danny said as he pulled another good print from the bar.

"Lucy's out back, checking another angle. She thinks she may have some DNA on some cigarette butts that she found in the woods near the back door."

Tate walked to the rear of the store where he observed the back door standing open. As he walked out the door, he could see Lucy taking photos of several cigarette butts on the ground between the woods and the door. It was about fifty feet from the store in some tall weeds that had been mashed down, as if someone had been crouched down in the area for a while.

"What's up, Lucy?"

"We did not get any prints on the back door or the front door, for what that's worth, but we know the perp entered the back door and surprised the victim from behind with the crowbar. We also think that he camped out here for at least thirty minutes to an hour where the cigarette butts are, and we know his DNA will be on the butts. We think he waited until no one else was in the store, then slipped up behind Tony and hit him with the crowbar."

"Lucy, I noticed that the crowbar happens to be an old and very used one, like maybe the perp brought it in with him."

"You may be right about that. Danny has been working with it and I think he's getting some good prints from it."

"Yes, Lucy, he's doing a good job... you both are."

Tate knows that the store is in an isolated area, with woods at the rear and a lazy street in front with very little traffic. So, it would be very easy for someone to park down the street or on a back road, walk through the woods to the rear of the store and wait until no one was inside but Tony. They could enter through the unlocked rear door, walk up behind Tony and do the deed. Or for that matter, they could have just as easily walked through the front door to accomplish their goal. But who? That is the big question. Yes, things are looking very good for the team, with these fingerprints and DNA from the cigarette butts. But to Tate, it just looks too easy... just too easy. Now, just when things could not get any better, another police officer radios that he has spotted a suspicious person in the area.

"Unit K-12 to command, I have an early model Dodge pick-up with a white male subject sitting in the driver's seat, while parked in the woods about two hundred yards from the crime scene at Johnson's store. The subject appears to be sleeping. Please advise, tag number KLMY429...10-28 and 10-27." (The officer has requested a tag registration and records check and a background on the owner through use of Ten Codes). A few minutes later the Command radios. "Command to K-12, vehicle comes back as a 1989 Dodge half-ton pick-up truck, registered to, Morton J. Ramsey, 719 Live Oak Street, Wilmington NC. The subject is a convicted felon... No outstanding at this time." After getting the information on Ramsey, the officer approached Ramsey and tapped on the side of the truck. At this time, Ramsey looked up from his sleep and asked,

"What's wrong officer?"

"Sir. Step out of the vehicle and keep your hands where I can see them."

"Yes Sir, whatever you say."

Ramsey has been through this before. He slowly opens the door and gets out of the truck with his hands up. He is about 6 feet tall, 185lbs, thin red hair with a five-day-old beard. He also looks much older than thirty-two years old. (The officer's registration check showed that he is only thirty-two years old.) His shirt and pants are dirty, and he looks and smells like he's not had a bath in over a week. A strong odor of cigarette smoke was all about him.

"Are you Mr. Ramsey? And may I see your driver's license and registration card?"

"Yes Sir." Ramsey reaches for his wallet in his front right pocket.
Ramsey is a carpenter by trade and has a drug addiction.   In the rear of the pick-up is a large toolbox that is full of tools, and several empty beer cans and whiskey bottles. There are also several loose tools in the bed of the truck. One more thing that was noticed that might be very significant later, but now looks unimportant, is that there are several cigarette butts on the ground next to the driver's side of the truck. Ramsay had smoked all these cigarettes.

"What are you doing out here?" The officer asked,

"I come over here almost every day, except the days that I am working and that's not very often. I am not bothering anyone. It's nice over here and I like it." Ramsey replied.

"Do you have any weapons or drugs on you or inside the vehicle?"

"No Sir, you can search me and my truck if you want to."

The officer gets a radio call from one of the CSI Investigators asking him to hold Ramsey for questioning regarding the murder of Johnson. When Ramsey heard the radio, he seemed very surprised.

"Who has been murdered? I did not kill nobody. No, I don't know anything about any murder." Ramsey said with a frantic look on his face.

"Sir, I am sorry, but you will have to come with me to the station. They want to talk with you."

Tate can hear all of what is going on and is very surprised. Somehow, Tate instinctively knew that the fingerprints on the crowbar and the DNA on the cigarette butts will belong to Ramsey. But he still knows that something is just not right. Where's the motive? Tate has a gut feeling that Ramsey has no motive. Within an hour, Tate is questioning Morton Ramsey down at the police department. He has been advised of his rights, and Ramsey stated that he was just sleeping off a buzz, so he would not cause an accident on the road.

"Sure, I knew Tony, everyone knows

Tony."

"Okay Mr. Ramsey, but…one question…
How did your crowbar, with your
fingerprints all over it, manage to crush the
back of Tony's head in?!"

"I don't know! Someone is trying to pin it
on me. I don't know why!"
Tate took a long hard look at Ramsey and
asked;

"Who would do this to you and why?"

"I don't know! I just don't know!"
Tate tells Ramsey;

"You will be charged with first-degree
murder and you will be convicted. So, if you
got any idea who wants your ass, you better
give it up and you better get a move on!"

"I don't know!! I tell you!"

"Okay, let's start with the very first thing
you did this morning." Tate asked.

"…I got up early…about 6:45 a.m."

"Then what?"

"I got dressed and drove to the McDonald's
down the road from Tony's store, to get some
breakfast."

"What time was that?"

"About 7:30 a.m. or so, I don't remember!"

"What did you do after you ate?"

"A fellow was supposed to call me about a job. I waited for a while, and I never got the call. So, that's when I drove over to where I was picked up by the police officer. When I got there, I got high on some PCP that I had. The next thing I knew, the officer was tapping on the window to my truck, and that's all I know!"

Chapter three

In Tate's mind, something was still just not right. So, with the District Attorney (DA) pushing for him to press charges and getting no place with Ramsey. He leaves the office headed back to Johnson's Hardware Store. By now the area has been cleared, and the body removed to the Medical Examiners Lab. Now back at the scene, Tate heads to the rear of the store, to the area where the cigarette butts were found. While standing there in deep thought, a hundred things going through his mind. He gets that old feeling… that feeling in his gut…not that police detective hunch, but that feeling he gets when he has got to get to a commode and in a hurry. You see… Tate has Irritable Bowel Syndrome (IBS) and when he has got to go, he's got to GO. He always carries a handful of toilet paper in his pocket for emergencies and this is a big one. He looks for the thickest spot in the woods that he can find, and he heads there as fast as he can. There is no one in the area at the time and he manages to get his pants down in the nick of time. Man, that was close. When he does the 'job' and the 'paperwork' has been completed, he heads back toward the cigarette butts.

As he's walking back toward the store, he realized that he has stepped in another large pile that someone else has left. And it was fresh, very fresh. After trying to clean his shoe with leaves, grass, and sticks, he realizes that his unfortunate step requires further action. Again, Tate had that instinctive feeling that he should get a sample from the feces. Although he is disgusted and somewhat sick to his stomach from the smell, Tate more closely examines the pile of poop. He spots what looks like a jellybean. He then takes an evidence bag from his pocket and manages to get a portion of feces, along with the jellybean, into the bag. Tate is thinking, *how crazy he must be to be doing this. Here he is digging in a pile of poop, that probably has absolutely nothing to do with the case…but what if it does?* It suddenly pops into Tate's head… *Tony has a small jar of red jellybeans on the counter in the store. And just maybe the perpetrator had been in Tony's store the day before…ate some jellybeans… and today he or she took a poop in the woods, and an undigested jellybean just happen to pass through??* Tate's really beginning to think he's lost his mind. He heads out of the woods toward the front of the building where Tony's car is located. A police officer is sitting in a patrol car next to Tony's car.

"Officer, have you been here all afternoon, sitting by this car?"

"Yes Sir."

"Has anyone been in the car?"

"No Sir, no one has been around the car." Tate opened the door and took the McDonald's receipt off the seat and puts it in another evidence bag. He continued to search the rest of the car but was unable to find any further evidence. Aggravated that there was no other significant evidence, Tate left for the McDonald's located at 1202 Old

Bridge Road, Wilmington, NC. He arrived, parked and ran inside.

"I need to see the manager." Tate said to one of the workers.

"He's in the back, I'll get him." The employee said. In a minute or so, the manager (a skinny young man) came out and asked;

"What is that smell!?" He then said; "Man I think you have got poop on you, man that's bad!"

"Look, don't worry about the smell, I am Detective Logan with the police department, and I need to see your videotapes from this morning."

"Ok, but you're going to have to get the poop off your shoe first." After Tate cleaned his shoe, the two went into a room in the back and the manager pulled the tape. The manager rewound the videotape to the time of 7:28 AM. It was about two minutes before Tony always came in for breakfast, and it was also two minutes before the time on the receipt. They could see Tony drive up, park and come into the store. He walked up to the counter, ordered. After they gave Tony his food, he walked over to a table and sat down to eat. Nothing suspicious. Tate also saw Ramsey drive up, park his old truck and walk into the store.

He, just like Tony, walked up to the counter, ordered, got his food and sat down. The two never made eye contact or even appeared to have noticed each other. Now, this was strange. But what Tate was about to see was very strange. One of the cameras that was taping Ramsey's truck, shows a tall thin well-dressed man walk up to the truck, reach over into the bed and remove a three-foot-long crowbar. He then walked away and out of camera view. But the way he picked up the crowbar was even stranger. He picked it up on the very end, on the hook end.

"I will need a copy of this tape and if possible, I also would like to take it with me." Tate stated.

"Sure, you can take this one and I will plug a new one into the recorder. Is there anything else I can do?"

"No thank you, this will help me a lot."

Tate leaves the McDonald's headed to the Medical Examiner's Office. By now, an autopsy was most likely underway on the body of his friend. When he arrived, he went into the procedure room and stood by the doctor. In most homicide cases, it's customary that the police detective that's handling the case sits in on the autopsy. It is a gross and gruesome ordeal. It is bad enough when it's a stranger, but it is very bad when the person happens to be your best friend. Tate was able to endure this, as hard as it was.

As Tate was standing there his mind goes back once more to the early years of his friendship with Tony. His mind drifted to the boot camp days they had spent at Fort Jackson, South Carolina. It was near the end of their basic training and they were doing hand-to-hand combat. The instructor would show them how to disarm someone that had a knife or a weapon. They also learned how to overcome them with a swift blow to the face. It sure looked easy when the instructor performed the moves on one of the soldiers.

The instructor was a seasoned sergeant. He was stout, weathered, and gruff. It's no telling how many times he had called these drills, which he probably did in his sleep.

"Now men! Do as I do! Take your right hand and your left hand up quickly, in front of you in a rigid position, and at the same time, stomp your left foot on the ground, and yell Hahhh!!" Now once more, as he does this, all fifty men do it with him. The loud voices from the men sound off. "Hahhh!!" They all throw their hands up and stomp their feet.

"Now men, this move will throw the enemy off and you will have the element of surprise on your side!"
Now, it seemed easy and we are the best of the best, or so we are told every day. Yes Sir, we are a bunch of fighting machines. Tate and Tony are thinking about what they have heard, as they are marching back to the barracks. Once at the barracks, everyone is dismissed for the weekend. Tony and Tate can't wait to get into Jacksonville to have some fun.

The first stop was the Desoto Bar. It was a hot spot for soldiers on the weekend. The bar was already loaded up with people drinking and having a good time. A draft beer, in one of those tall skinny glasses was on special for just fifty cents a glass. It looked good, but with the foam three inches thick and only three more inches of beer in the bottom of the glass, it gave you about four ounces of beer. Just to even get a buzz, you would have to drink twenty or more of them. By then, you were broke. Anyway, Tate and Tony were having a grand old time. It started getting late and Tate decided to get one more draft from the bar before they left for the post. As Tate squeezed in at the bar, he accidently spilled his beer on, of all people the drill sergeant, who has been teaching hand-to-hand combat all week. This upset the old guy so bad that he got up and spun Tate around and drew back to let him have one. But the quick-thinking Tate, remembered all that training. He threw his hands up and stomped his left foot on the floor and yelled, "Hahhh!!" The next thing

Tate knew, he had been knocked completely across the room and landed under a table. With blood flowing from his nose, he looked up to see that just about everyone in the bar, are brawling in a bar room fight. People, chairs, tables, beer glasses and bottles flew all over the bar. He saw Tony right in the thick of things, fighting as hard as he could. Men were knocked to the floor, one after the other. Tony has even knocked that old drill sergeant out! It was not long before the Military Police (MP) came running in breaking up the fight.

Later that night back on base, the head MP came into the brig to see Tony.

"Soldier, I could not help but see you in that bar. I must admit, you are the best that I have ever seen when it comes to fighting. You will be out of basic training in a week and I want you to come in with me as an MP."

Tony just stood there for a minute and looked at Tate.

"What about my friend? Can he come too?" Tony said, as he pointed toward Tate.

"Well, just who is your friend? Stand up soldier!" The MP Sergeant said as he walked over to Tate.

"Yes Sir!" Tate said as he quickly jumped to attention, with blood all over his shirt and face.

"So, you come as a team. Well, to get him, I will take you too. But you are going to have to do better in the future. We can't have our MP's getting beat up all the time."

"Tate...Tate...Tate! Snap two, you were a million miles from here. What were you thinking?" Doc said, as he poked Tate in the side with his elbow.

"What's the outcome Doc?" Tate asked.

"The force from the crowbar was the cause of death, plain and simple. He never knew what hit him. Death came very quickly." Dr. Orwell was a well-known pathologist that had conducted hundreds of autopsies.

"Look Doc, I have something else I need to check out and I know you can do it."

"Alright Tate, I am almost afraid to ask, but what is it?"

He pulls the bag of poop out of his pocket

and shows it to the Doctor.

"What? No, is that…what I think it is?"

"Yes, it is. And I really need you to get a DNA test run on it. I found it at the crime scene and I just have the strangest feeling that it is somehow involved in the case."

"Tate this had better be good, you know the District Attorney would be raising hell if he knew you were pulling this stunt on a hunch."

"Doc, if this works out the DA will be good with it, and if not then it's on me."

"Haha, you can say that again. It may take me a few hours, but I'll get to it today or no later than tomorrow morning. And Tate, his wallet had over three thousand dollars in it." Tate took one more look at his old friend and sadly left the area, heading back to the station to continue questioning Ramsey. On the drive back, all kinds of things were going through his mind. *Who and why? Motive…there was none. Revenge…no way. It just made no sense. No sense at all.* This would be the hardest case of his life.

Chapter four

As Tate walked into Brad's office, he could tell that Brad was extremely upset and on edge, to say the least.

"Tate! Where the hell have you been? The DA is having a fit! He wants Ramsey charged. The prints on the crowbar and the DNA on the cigarette butts have come back to Ramsey. He needs to be charged!"

"Brad! Ramsey did not kill Tony! You have to see this videotape." The two went into the video room and Tate plugged it in. When Captain Carter saw it, he was speechless.

"How did you come up with this? This changes everything, but it's not going to work with the DA. He will say, 'so what,' someone took a tool from a killer's vehicle. That has nothing to do with this." (The DA is a hard-driving ambitious white male, about thirty-seven years old with a lot of education, and no common sense.)

Tate left the office and headed back to the McDonald's. In his mind, he knows he has a lot to do in a very short amount of time. He needed to find out who the tall, thin, well-dressed man is, because he knows that this is the perpetrator. In no time, he's at McDonald's and as he looks across the street, he spots a gas station. If they have cameras, then he may find more footage of that suspicious thin man. He drove over, and he could see several cameras located on the outside of the building. Once inside, he asked to speak to someone that could show him the footage on the cameras. The manager invited him in and on the monitors, he observed one camera that shows part of the McDonald's parking lot. When the tape was rolled back to 7:28 AM, you could see Tony's car drive into the McDonald's lot. You could even see Tony go toward the front door before he went out of view. Then, Ramsey's truck could be seen going into the lot and just like Tony, he went toward the door. A few other people went in and out of the building. Now, there it is. A very nice, late model Corvette pulled in and parked next to the road, closer to the camera. A tall thin, well dressed, white male got out and slowly walked towards Ramsey's truck. He seemed to be very cautious as he approached the rear of Ramsey's truck. He looked around, and then quickly grabbed the crowbar and headed back to his vehicle. He got back into the Vette and left the area, headed in the direction of Johnson's Hardware Store. Tate grabbed the tape and left the area headed toward Tony's store.

Now, Tate has a little more on the suspect, but he has a lot more work ahead. It's about three miles from the McDonald's to Tony's store, Tate drives very slowly. As he is driving, he is looking for other cameras in other store lots that may have captured the suspicious thin man in his Vette. If he could discover the tag number, it would help. After all, a bright shiny new Corvette stands out like a flashing neon sign.

While on the way to Tony's, Tate reports the new information to Captain Carter. He also asked if he could run a DMV (Department of

Motor Vehicles), search on every late-model Corvette registered in this area. Carter once again tells Tate he would do whatever he could, but they are running out of time. It's getting late and Tate hasn't got anything else. Now Tate's getting a call from Dr. Orwell.

"Tate there were two different DNA samples in the poop."

"What...? how could that be?"

"Tate, that thing you thought was a jellybean just happened to be the end of a human pinky finger. I am looking through our DNA files to see who these samples might come back to, but you know how that works. They may not be in the database. I will let you know if I find anything else. Oh, hold on a minute, that finger belongs to an unidentified female. The sample from the poop belongs to an unidentified male subject."

"The Captain is holding the DA off for another few hours, but I am running out of time. So, please work with me on this."

"Okay Tate, I'll do what I can."

Tate knows he's got a live wire on his hands, and who knows what's coming next?

As Tate's phone rings, and he reaches over to answer it, he thinks. *Now, who could this be?* It's the skinny McDonald's manager. "Detective Logan, I helped you with that videotape this morning and I have a strange request. I don't know how to say this, but some guy came in this morning after you left. He handed me a note addressed to you."

"What was his name?"

"Sir, he would not give his name, he just gave this note with this phone number and written instructions on the note to tell you to call him at 5:00 p.m. today and not a minute sooner or later. The number is, 910-575-2000, and he never said a word."

"Thank you and by the way, what did he look like?"

"He was a tall skinny man, about six foot four, maybe 180 lbs. He is about forty years old and very well dressed. He had short dark hair that was neatly cut. He looked like someone that has a very good job. If you know what I am saying...and had dark skin, but he appears to be a white man."

"Thanks again for letting me know…oh did you see what he was driving?"

"No Sir, I did not. Oh, and he had gloves on."

Tate thought… *Man, this guy is playing with me. Who have I made so mad that he would kill my best friend and then play games with me about it?* Tate called one of the investigators at the phone company. Tate has a very good rapport with them. They had really helped him in the past.

"Bell Communications, Investigator White speaking, May I help you?"

"Tim, it's Tate, I need a big favor. Can you help me?"

"Sure Tate, what's up?"

"910-575-2000, who does it belong to?"

"Hold on a minute, I'll run it through the database."

"Thanks Tim, I will pay for lunch next time we get together."

"Tate, that's what you said the last time I ran a number for you. Hold on, here it is…comes back to a phone booth at 901

Southeast Street, Wilmington. And Tate it's one of the last payphone booths that's out there." Tate knew this guy is much too smart to be caught in a phone booth, but Tate will call it at 5:00 PM. Now, the Captain is calling.

"Tate, I think I've found the owner of the Vette you are looking for and the owner is mad as a hornet."

"Who is he and why is he mad? Oh, let me guess, the Vette has been stolen."

"You got it. Tate, you're dealing with a deranged nut case. Please be careful! He's after you for some reason. Keep me posted, and the DA is still on my case."

"Yeah and when he finds out what I have, he will come around. If not, I'll be wondering about him. Got to go, getting another call." It's the Medical Examiner.

"Hello, Doc have you got anything for me?"

"Yes, that female DNA from the finger comes back to a murder victim, by the name of Doris Dooly, you should remember her. As for the male DNA from the poop...no match."

"What? I got the guy that killed her, it was my last homicide case. It was just last month. You know it just hit me... her right pinky finger was missing. I can't believe that. How did the finger end up in the Thin Man's poop? And even worse, did we charge the wrong guy in that case?"

"You know, Tate you're going to have to bring all of this out and your time is short."

"I know that time is running out, but I am getting so close and we have to get this psycho off the street."

When the good Doctor hung up, the thought went through Tate's mind, *'Please don't tell me that I have already charged an innocent man in another murder case. Did this psycho frame someone else and now he's trying to do it again? Whoever this guy is, he is a very smart person. He is more than likely a serial killer that loves to play games with law enforcement. What's his next move? Either I have smoked him out, or he has smoked me out? Either way, the fight is now on and it will get worse at some point.* It is time to call

Brad and bring him up to speed on what's going on. Three rings and Brad picked the phone up and immediately started coming down on Tate.

"Tate you're running out of time!"

"I know, but this guy is a very sick serial killer. He wants me to call him today at 5:00 PM. The number is to a phone booth at 901 Southeast Street and I know he won't be there. And get this, I found a pile of poop in the woods at the crime scene and I had it checked for DNA. I did not find out who he is. However, it appears that he ate Doris Dooly's right pinky finger. It was in the poop that I submitted for a DNA test... Brad, we may have convicted an innocent man in that case."

"Oh no! What is going on here? Tate, I can't stall the DA any longer, we have to take this new evidence to him, then maybe he'll back off."

"Okay Brad, we need a unit on that phone booth before 5:00 PM. I will call that pay phone, but he will not be there. He's setting me up, I just don't know what he has in store."

"How did he contact you?"

"He gave the McDonald's manager a note to call me. Now, the manager has looked him right in the face. So, maybe we can get a good composite. I need to go back and look at the new tape, but I don't have time."

"I'll send someone to get the tape, don't worry about that."

"Okay, I have one more thing I need to do. I've got to go, thanks."

"What are you going to do?" Brad said as Tate hung up. Now, Brad is yelling into the phone at Tate, but Tate's gone. Tate knows that this guy is more than likely a wealthy person with lots of free time on his hands. He may live close, if not in the Wilmington area. He keeps a very low profile and is somewhat of a recluse, with a very high IQ. He is also a homicidal maniac that has killed many different people over the years. There is also a good chance that he's at the end of the line and he is up for his last big challenge. So, he feels he has nothing to lose.

Tate thinks this because he has shown himself to a possible witness (the McDonald's manager). On the other hand, he could be playing the role of the happy husband and father of three children. Only he holds this very sick and dark secret. Tate also knows, this guy has marked him. Somehow, Tate has got to put that mark back on the Thin Man.

Chapter five

5:00 PM:

The phone booth has been staked out by a plain clothes police officer in an unmarked police cruiser. Tate places the call. Tate is located one block away and is skeptical anyone will answer the telephone. The pay phone starts to ring. In the distance, the plain clothes officer notices a man walking slowly towards the phonebooth. As it rings, the man gets closer and closer. Now, at the booth, the man stopped, opened the door, stepped in and picked the phone up.

"Hello...Hello."

Tate being surprised by this said.

"Okay, you wanted me to call. Now, what?"

The man then said,

"You are to meet a fellow at the hotel on the waterway, Room 108. It faces the water. Knock on the door three times and you will

be given instructions on what to do."
He then hung the phone up. Tate radioed the officers near the phone booth to move in. The three unmarked police cars move in. Five plain clothes police officers jump out and take the unidentified man down. It's not the Thin Man. It is a street person by the name of Joe Applebee. (Joe is well known by the police, Joe is not completely 'all there' mentally, but he managed to handle this okay.)
Joe tells the police that someone paid him $50 to take the call and to give the instructions. The poor guy was scared out of his mind. Tate arrived about the time Joe had begun to settle down. Much to everyone's surprise, the pay phone starts to ring.

"All right, fellows, that's for me." Tate said as he stepped into the booth and picked up the phone receiver.

"Detective Logan, you egocentric, narcissist reprobate! Let the games begin! You thought you had me, but no, NO! You're just plain dumb and ignorant, and you don't have a clue! Ha ha ha ha ha!" (The caller's voice is disguised with a voice scrambler.)

Tate's blood is boiling, and he is about to lose it, but he knows it would not be in his best interest.

"Okay, 'Thin Man' you're doing pretty good. You are playing a good game here. But you have a big advantage over me. You know all about me and I only know what you look like. As a matter of fact, I've got a very good picture of you and it will be on the TV news all over the country. But really! That would be too easy. I want to get you one on one, that is if you think you're up to it. Let's cut to the chase."

The man on the phone said;

"No, you can't get me, you're just an old, washed-up detective. By the way, I also have IBS and I never thought you would find that pile I dropped near the cigarette butts. I must admit, that was good on your part. Let's see now, about two to three seconds left. Ha ha ha ha!" Then, click the phone goes dead. Tate knows he has just missed tracing the call by two seconds. Man, this guy is smart. Just two more seconds and he would have had a number. The Captain had done a good job tapping the pay phone and setting up a trace on the line as well, but they just fell a little short.

Tate knows it's a wash, but he and two more officers go to the hotel room as directed by Joe. They knock, and a little old lady comes to the door. Obviously, this was not connected, and these men knew it. They spoke to the lady and after a minute they left. Tate heads back to meet with the DA and Captain Carter. They are going to have to let Mr. Ramsey go. The DA is not happy, but he has no choice. As they were talking with Ramsey, he told them that he would go to the path behind the hardware store about two or three times a week. He would sit in his truck and get high on whatever he had. He would also smoke several cigarettes and throw the butts on the ground next to his truck.

"Did you ever see a tall thin, well-dressed man in the area?" Tate asked.

"No Sir, I never saw anyone like that. No,

wait, I did see a man like that in the hardware store one day."

"Do you remember when you saw him?"

"It was about a week ago, he was in a heated conversation with Tony. I don't know what they were talking about. The minute they saw me, they stopped talking and the tall, thin, well- dressed guy left the store."

"Did you see what he was driving?"

"No, I sure didn't."

"Okay, sorry about having to bring you in, but I'm sure you understand why. If you see or hear anything, please let us know."

This new information may turn everything on its ear. Now if, in fact, the Thin Man knew Tony, this could change everything. But how could they prove a connection? Then, it hit him…

"Brad, I would like to pull Tony's phone records for the past two months. We may find the 'Thin Man' through the records."

"Sure, get on it, but keep me posted." The Captain said. They all head home for the evening. But the next day doesn't come quickly for Tate. A long, sleepless night with thoughts of losing his best friend and the imminent threat from the 'Thin Man' are looming over him like the grim reaper.

Chapter six

8:01 AM, Wednesday, August 4, 2007:

Tate's walking into his office, and at the
same time he's requesting phone records
from Tony's cell phone, home phone and
business phone. It will take about three
hours for the records to come in, so Tate will
meet with the DA and his Captain about the
investigation. A few minutes later, with
coffee in hand, the meeting is beginning.
The DA is still upset about this case, The
Captain is somewhat stoic, and Tate is very
quiet.

"Tate, you and your piles of poop and some
suspicious 'Thin Man,' is about to take me
over the edge! What are you going to come
up with next? We look like a bunch of fools,
thanks to you. We had all the proof we
needed to charge Ramsey and now we have
nothing! Nothing!"
Tate just sat there saying nothing and staring
into his cup of coffee. Captain Carter stood

up and said;

"Look we had no choice but to let Ramsey go. Sure, the crowbar was his and sure his fingerprints were all over it. And yes, given the cigarette butts with his DNA on each one, made it look like it was Ramsey. But now we have the videotape of the 'Thin Man' taking the crowbar from Ramsey's truck. Also, the admission from him, that he killed Tony and set Ramsey up… we had no other choice. Don't forget about the DNA of the little finger that was in the feces. That DNA was that of a previous murder victim. So, not only was he about to frame Ramsey, but there is a guy sitting in jail, who may have been wrongly convicted of murdering the woman with the missing finger. So, it looks like we need to be thanking Tate and not chastising him."

As Carter was giving his speech to the DA, Tate just sits there staring into his coffee, saying nothing.

Now, the DA said;

"Okay, Captain Carter, do what you need to do, but get this thing wrapped up, and soon!" He then stormed out of the room.

"Okay, Tate I know you've got this, but please be careful! Stay in close contact with me. As a matter of fact, you need to get out of your place and stay somewhere the Thin Man can't find you. I don't want to have to investigate your murder."

All Tate could say was:

"Are we through here?"

"Yes, please be careful." Brad said with a sigh.

The two left the room heading back to their offices. As Tate walked in, his phone started to ring.

"Detective Logan, Can I help you?"

"Tate, your phone records are in. Do you want to come over or shall I bring them to you?"

"No Sally, I'll come over and pick them up, thanks."

On the way over, he stopped by the Captain's office.

"Brad, I am going to get the facial composite artist to work with the Manager at McDonald's to see if we can get a face for the Thin Man."

"Tate, you may want to get him hooked up with Ramsey as well."

"I don't know Brad, from what Ramsey told us, he never really saw the Thin Man's face, but I'll set' em up anyway."
After stopping by the facial composite guy's office, Tate stopped by Sally's office to get the phone records.

"Tate, here they are, two months' worth. If you need any more just give me a call, and if you find any suspicious phone numbers while going through these records, just call."

"Okay Sally, I will."

"Tate, the word is out about the danger in this case. Please be careful."

"Sally, some people around here have big mouths. Don't believe everything you hear."
As he walked out of her office, he looked around at Sally and they give each other a wink and a smile. Tate knows this case will be very difficult and even though he plays it off, he knows it could get him killed. The phone records were all over the place. Tate knows that his phone numbers will be all

through the records. Several other numbers
in the reports are known to Tate and are not
suspicious. Suddenly, he spots one number
that grabs him like a bolt from the blue…
910-575-2000. It's that pay phone. A call
was made at about the time Ramsey saw the
'Thin Man' in the store.
Now, why would this be and what was Tony
and the 'Thin Man' arguing about? Tate's
mind is racing. *Cameras! I wonder if there
are some cameras around the phonebooth?*
Tate springs to his feet and hurries to his car.
He drives to the pay phone and starts looking
for a business with outside cameras.   Out of
luck… no camera. The air in Tate's sails
quickly dissipates. It is back to square one.
Now, the only hope is that the composite
facial artist can produce a face.
All day Tate struggles with this case. His
blood pressure seems to be going up by the
minute. But that is just in his mind, Tate's in
outstanding physical shape and his blood
pressure, historically, has never been high. It
was nerve-racking.
The next day, after another sleepless night,

Tate is on the way to his office when he gets the call from the composite facial artist.

"Tate, good news, I was able to get a very good face for you!"

"Great, I am on the way, see you in about five minutes." Then, just like he said, Tate comes racing through the door, all worked up.

"What have you got, my good man?"

"Tate, here it is, the McDonald's manager came through, but the drug addict had nothing." As Tate looks at the picture, he takes a big sigh.

"Man, this is like gold to me, we've got him now! Thank you! Thank you!"

"Call me anytime Tate, and please be careful."

Tate is now on a roll, and he has another idea related to the phone booth and the call that was made to Tony's store. What if the 'Thin Man' had gone to the phone booth to get the phone number for Tony's store?! Tate calls Lucy in CSI.

"Lucy, this is Tate and I need a big favor."

"Okay Tate, what can I do for you today?"

"Lucy, I need you to go with me to a phone booth to see if you can get a fingerprint from a page in the phone book."

"Sure, let me get my kit."

"Thanks, Lucy, I'll swing by and pick you up."

Chapter seven

10:38 AM, Thursday, August 5, 2007:

Tate and Lucy arrive at the phone booth.
The phone book is hanging on a chain inside
the booth.
   "Tate, what do you want me to work on?"
Tate steps into the booth and carefully opens
the yellow pages to *Johnson's Hardware
Store*, then said to Lucy;
   "You see the number to the hardware
store."
   "Yes, I see it."
Tate continued,
   "Lucy, when a person makes a call, do you
think that they would place their right or left
index finger under the number as they were
dialing it?"
   "Tate, you're right, let me see if there is a
print there."
After dusting the area, she pulled a perfect
print.
   "I got a good one Tate, but who knows who

it will come back to."

"Well Lucy, Tony did not get a lot of calls, and so far, only one came from this phone. Now, we can only hope that the print is on file somewhere."

Tate and Lucy left the area headed back to the police station. Tate had high hopes that the print will bring a suspect to light. Now, it's a waiting game once more. The 'Thin Man' may not be as smart as he thinks he is. While back at the station, Tate brings the Captain up to speed on the fingerprint. They both are feeling good about the print. So, it's back to work on several other cases that are in the works. Unlike TV Cops, that only have one case at the time, in the real world, an investigator may have as many as twenty to thirty cases to investigate at one time. The day goes fast but the night drags on. Another long night for Tate and he is back in the office.

9:38 AM, Friday, August 6, 2007:

When Tate's phone rings. It's Lucy the CSI officer.

"Tate, I have good news, and bad news, on that fingerprint."

"Give me the good news first."

"We know who the print comes back too. Now, the bad news, the print was from the right index finger of George W. Wilson." Tate was speechless. This finger came from another murder victim. Wilson was reported missing on Sunday, June 1, 2007, and was found dead on the side of the road on June 3rd, 2007 and his right index finger had been removed.

"No! No! The 'Thin Man' has struck again. He's playing with me!"

"No, Tate he's playing with all of us. He's making us look like fools."

"Lucy, we are dealing with the smartest person I have ever seen in my life. The composite is due to air on the local news tonight and maybe that will get 'em. I am hoping that someone will come forward, so we can get him off the street."

After talking with Lucy, Tate called Captain Carter.

"Brad, you're not going to believe me…but that print from the yellow pages…"

"Yes, What about it? Is it on file?"

"Yes, Brad, it's on file alright."

"Well, man! Tell me about it!"

"I will, but it's not going to make you feel any better about this case."

"For God's sake! Tate. Tell me about it."

Tate tells Brad and Brad is beside himself with disbelief.

"Okay, Tate, I know that composite will be hitting the news tonight and I really hope that we'll get a hit. The composite has also been distributed to all the patrol and detective units."

Tate asked,

"Brad, do you think it would be a good idea for someone to talk with the owner of the stolen Vette? The owner may have seen a person fitting the description of the Thin Man. You know, he may have a clue for us."

"No Tate, the only time the guy was talked

to, was when the officer took the report."

"Hmmm… I need to get that police report, because I would like to talk with that fellow." After talking with Brad, Tate pulled the report and called the victim of the stolen Vette. The man was a little apprehensive about meeting with Tate. He told Tate,

"You people are not doing a good job and I don't have time to meet with a bunch of losers. Just find the car and leave me alone." So, Tate backed off and did not pursue the matter any further. He did think the owner's response was somewhat suspicious.

Chapter eight

1:00 PM

As Tate looks at his watch… he knows that he must attend an event today that he wished was not happening. It's Tony's memorial service. It's at 2:00 PM and Tate's going to be there for his friend's farewell. So, he tells Brad that he will be 10-7 (out of service) from 1:30 PM to about 3:30 PM for Tony's funeral today.

As Tate pulls into the parking lot at Forest Gardens Memorial Grounds, only good thoughts are on his mind. He's thinking of some of the good times that he's had with his friend over the many years. He can see and hear Tony telling some of those crazy jokes he knew. He can't forget the taste of that Italian food that Tony used to cook for everyone at his house on all those Saturday nights. *'Man, he was a good cook.'*

At the service, Tate can see Tony's sister and many family friends. Some have even come from Italy. With most everyone dressed in black and standing by the gravesite, Tony's Pastor is reading the 23rd Psalm. It's a solemn and sad event. Tate is holding back tears for Tony. When all the formalities ended, everyone walked from the gravesite over to a fellowship hall for some refreshments and a time to remember Tony's life.

Tate stood with many of Tony's friends and family, some that he had never seen before. He met *Uncle Louie*. Tate has heard all the funny stories about him over the years. He had heard some of them a hundred times, but he loved to hear Tony tell them. Uncle Louie must be in his 90's, but he looked good for his age. Now, unlike, at the grave site, everyone appeared to be very happy. It was like they were having a big party. It was not like he thought it would be, no, not at all. It was something that Tate would not forget anytime soon. They all laughed, talked, drank wine and told even more stories about Tony. It was a great time for Tate and everyone else at the gathering. Tate said goodbye to the family and headed back to work. Tate like many others would miss Tony very much.

As Tate was leaving, he spotted a woman outside, with her back to the door. She was a blonde and she was smoking a cigarette. He could not see her face, but he recognized her. He had seen her many times in the past, but it was several years ago. He stopped behind the woman and called her name… "Mary Ann." Hearing his voice, she quickly turned around. "Tate! Oh Tate! I had to come, but I just can't go in there!" She dropped her cigarette to the sidewalk and reaches out to hug Tate.

"Mary Ann, why don't you go in? I know his family would like to see you."

"Tate, when I heard, I just could not believe it…"

"Yes, Mary Ann, it is hard for all of us. But we will have to deal with what has happened."

"His sister, Maria called me the day it happened. She also called me back with the information about the funeral. I think the world of Maria, and we have kept in contact all these years."

"And you know she's in there. So, why don't you go on in?"

"I wish I had never left 'em, I still love 'em, but I knew I couldn't live this slow country way. He would not change. Oh, I wish I could get a do-over on this. But I know…"

"You know Mary Ann; you have not changed one little bit. You still look the same as you did years ago. You know, he never remarried…and he kept your picture by his bed. He always loved you."

"You're not going to believe me when I tell you… I remarried a man that I truly love. But he's not like Tony, at all. We met in New York. He's an accounting manager that makes a lot of money. The funny thing about it all is that we moved to a little country town in the south that's even smaller than Wilmington. So much for the big city life. Oh, and I also have three children; two girls and a boy, and they all have grown up and moved out."

"Mary Ann, life does have a way of throwing us all a curve once in a while."

"Tate, Maria also told me years ago about you and Susan. By the way, do you know how she is doing?"

"Oh, Susan's doing just fine. She's remarried to a city employee. He is an office worker. She seems to be very happy. I see her occasionally."

"Tate, who could have done this to Tony? It makes no sense."

"I know Mary Ann, and I am the one that will catch whoever did this to Tony. I have got to get the low life piece of crap! Somehow, I am going to get 'em, if it's the last thing I do!"

"I sure hope you do!"

"Now Mary Ann, come on in to see the family and friends. Come on…I will even go in with you."

"No, Tate, I can't do it. I felt the resentment as I drove up and parked. I just can't do it."

"All right Mary Ann, do what you have to do, but I know you are going to regret this in the end."

After a moment of deep thought, she turned and walked toward her car. Tate knew that she was in agony over this. So, he runs after her.

"Wait! Don't leave like this!"

"Tate, I have to get the heck out of here!" She said with tears running down her face.

"Okay Mary Ann, I understand, but before you leave town, let's go someplace and have a cup of coffee. We'll talk about the good times we all had. I think it will make your trip back home a little easier."

"Okay Tate, you make the call. Where to?"

"Mary Ann, do you remember that little Italian place over on 29th. street?"

"How could I ever forget that hole in the wall? It was Tony's favorite place to go and the food was pretty good too."

"Okay, get in my car and that is where we are going. I just can't let you run out without at least catching up a little. After all, Tony would never have forgiven me, if I didn't try to comfort you at a time like this." Now, as they are headed to the restaurant, Mary Ann starts to tell Tate a story about the last few days she spent with Tony. "Tate, three days before I left Tony, I had an affair with another man. I just don't know what came over me. I did not even like the guys looks. It was just one of those crazy things, and I have lived with that for years. Then, a week after I got back to New York, I started having morning sickness. Oh, I was sure that I had let that fool of a man get me pregnant. I just did not know…sure Tony and I had been having unprotected sex. We had even been talking about having children. And, I wanted the baby to be Tony's. But I just did not know, and I was so ashamed. That's why I never came back."

"Mary Ann everyone makes mistakes… Tony would have understood… He loved you that much."

"Yes…He may have forgiven me, and he may have killed that fool of a man too."

"How did it turn out…I mean you and the baby and everything?"

"Tate I never heard from the man with whom I had the affair. I also met a man that

I thought I could love. He knew that I was pregnant, and he did not even care. He asked me to marry him about three weeks after we met. I knew that I would have to get a divorce from Tony. But when I got to looking at our marriage papers, I discovered that we, where not really married. It seems that the papers, had not been done right. So, there was no need to get a divorce. So, we got married before I started showing and I had that baby. It was a boy…and the minute it popped out I knew that it was Tony's." Then she broke down once more.

"Tony never knew that he had a son, and that boy turned out to be the best thing!"

"Mary Ann, there was nothing else you could do…" Tate said as he tried to comfort her.

"Now, you see why I could not go in there, don't you?"

"Yes Mary Ann, I understand. Tony used to say that he wished he could have had a real family. But you or no one else can go back in time, and change things like we want it to be. It is what it is."

"Tate, please don't ever tell anyone about this. Bill, my husband, loves Anthony, that's what I named my first born. Bill knows who his son is named after, and he's never said a word. He loves him just as much as if he was his own and that's the way we both look at it all. Now, some day little Tony may find out and if he does, it's going to rip my heart out. I just pray that this never comes out. You understand, don't you?"

"Mary Ann, no one will ever know... I give you my word. After all, what possible good would come from anyone finding out?"

"Tate, I need to be getting back. You understand."

They never got to the restaurant. Tate just drove around while talking with Mary Ann. Tate knew that going into the restaurant, was not a good idea. So, he drives her back to her car at the funeral home. They both get out and Tate walks Mary Ann to her vehicle. She got in and drove away. Not even a good-bye. She was broken hearted for sure. Tate understood. As she drove off into the distance, Tate could not help but to have deep sorrow for Mary Ann. There is nothing he can do.

All those years and Tony never knew that he had a son. Anthony would have been loved by his Dad more than life. He was the missing link that would have changed everything in Tony's life. What a shame, it had to end like this. Why couldn't things have been different? Just goes to show just how much one little mistake can change everything. Poor, Mary Ann…has had to live with this and now she will never have any peace. If only she had told Tony, things might have been quite different now. It would have been very difficult for Mary Ann to confess, but the result might be much better now. It's way too late to back up now.

Chapter nine

6:00 PM

Tate has his TV on, and he is anxious to see the news with the composite drawing of the Thin Man. He is on standby just in case someone calls the hotline number at the police station. His hopes are running high. Now here it is, on TV for thousands of people to see. Surely, someone will know who this guy is. Tate is ready, willing and able to put the cuffs on the Thin Man and close this case out for good. After the news aired, several calls came in, but the call that ended up being the most helpful was from an off-duty police officer. The off-duty officer, David Miller, just happened to be the officer that took the call about the stolen Corvette. Tate took off for the police department to meet with Officer Miller. When he arrived, Miller is sitting in his office. Tate walked in and showed him the composite sketch of the Thin Man.

"Tell me about this picture. How do you know this person?"

"I understand that the composite just went out today, and I was off duty. So, I didn't get to see it until tonight on the news. I know who this guy is."

"That's great, who is it?" Tate asked.

"It's the guy that reported the stolen Corvette, James D. Waters. I know that face and here is the report that gives all the information on him." Tate was shocked once more.

"I also have a copy of the report, and I called the guy this afternoon and requested to meet with him. I thought he may have some information on a murder case we've been working on. Now I can see why the lousy rascal blew me off."

At this time, the Captain came bursting into Tate's office.

"Tate, I just heard! It looks like we got the son of a gun! Let's get the team out there and pick' em up before he makes a run for it! We are also, getting search warrants for his house." Tate looks at Officer Miller as they are rushing from his office, and said,

"Yeah, news really travels fast around here!"

7:05 PM

And the team has assembled and are ready to go.

"Tate we've got to be careful, this is one dangerous man," the Captain said as they hurried out the door. All the way to this guy's house, all Tate could think was, *this is too easy, something is just not right. How could the smartest person he had ever seen make such a big mistake?* As they approached, about two miles from James D. Waters' house, they started running silent, no blue lights or siren. When they arrived at the house, they split up. Half of the group went to the rear and the other half to the front. This house is lavish and in a wealthier section of town. A quick police background check shows that Waters is a white male, forty-one years old, 6'4' and 170lbs, blue eyes, with brown hair.

Tate and the Captain do not have an arrest warrant, so they must be careful.   They want to question him with the intention of charging him. Tate knocked and rang the doorbell at the front door. After a minute or two, Waters slowly opens the door.

"What do you want?"

"Are you James D. Waters?" Tate replied.

"Yes, I am, now who are you?"

"My name is Detective Tate Logan, with the Wilmington Police Department, and we need to talk with you. We also have a search warrant to search your property."

"What do you want to talk to me about?"

"Sir, you're going to have to come down to the station because you have been identified as a suspect in a murder case." Tate and the Captain had enough to take him in for questions, but they didn't have enough to make the arrest. So, they were walking a tightrope. Much to Tate and Captain's surprise, Waters was willing to go. As they leave the area, the team starts searching the property. The ride to the station with Tate, the Captain, and Waters was very quiet.

8:03 PM

They all are now at the station. Waters is placed in the interrogation room and just like all interrogation rooms, there is a one-way glass. As Waters sits in the room alone, he appears cool and collected. Tate walks into the room, while the Captain and the DA look on through the one-way glass. Tate sits in a chair across the table from Waters, and he just glares at Waters.
After a minute Waters said;
    "I thought you wanted to ask me some questions, why are you just sitting there?"
Tate starts his line of questions.
    "Did you happen to see the 6:00 PM news tonight?"
    "No."
Tate pulled the composite of the Thin Man out and placed it in front of Waters and said;
    "Who is this?"
    "Hmmm… It looks like me, doesn't it?"
    "Yes, it looks just like you. Mr. Waters, do you know Tony Johnson, and have you ever been to Johnson's Hardware Store?"

"Sure, I know Tony and I have been to the store. Why?"

"Waters stop this game you're playing… we've got you; the game is over!!"

Waters looked at Tate and said.

"Look I did not have to come down here with you and if I am not under arrest, I want you to take me back home."

Now, Tate was in a corner.

"Look! We have you on videotape at the McDonald's taking the crowbar from Ramsey's pick-up truck. The manager can identify you, and you were also seen in the Corvette the same day at McDonald's when you took the crowbar. The game is over!"

"I have never even been to a McDonald's. I can't eat that crap. There's no way, what have I got to do to make you understand! I don't know what you are talking about!"

"Okay, there is one thing that you could do that would convince me."

"Alright, what have I got to do?"

"You need to give me a sample of your DNA."

"No! No! I will not do it; I have not done

anything and now I want to see my lawyer!"
At this point, Tate leaves the room and
Captain Carter walks in and sits down.

"Mr. Waters, would you like a smoke or a
drink?"

"No, I want my lawyer."

"You can call your lawyer anytime you
want, I just want to ask you one more
question. Is that okay?"

"I don't know what you people are talking
about. Sure, I knew the guy and I have even
had some problems with him, but I never
killed him!"

"What kind of problems did you have with
Mr. Johnson and when was that?"

"Oh, it was about two weeks ago, I stopped
by the store to pick up a special part that he
was supposed to have ordered for me. When
I went in, he blew me off by saying that I
never told him to order that part. So, I was
upset, and I let him have it, but that was the
end of it! I left and forgot about the whole
thing. It was over for me." Tate came back
into the room with three diet cokes.

"Here you are guys, have a coke, and

everyone, just settle down."

"I want my lawyer!"

"Sure, you can call your lawyer, we just have one more question. Right, Captain?"

"Sure, just one more question. I'll tell you what, if you do one thing, just one thing for us we will take you back home."

"What's that?"

"We have someone that needs to look at you and if this person tells us that he has never seen you, you're home free. Now if that's okay, that will be all. I mean it, just one more thing and then you can go."

"Okay, let's get it over with," as he took a drink of Diet Coke.

The manager from McDonald's was there to see a lineup and to see if he could identify Waters as the Thin Man. The battle is almost over. They can proclaim Waters as a suspect and advise him of his rights, push for DNA, and then make an arrest. A few minutes later, Waters walked out with five other people of similar build and appearance. As they stood there, the manager came out and took a good look at each person. After a few minutes, he points to Waters. At this point, Waters is taken back into the interrogation room. Upon returning to the interrogation room something was missing. Yes, the Diet Coke can that Mr. Waters was drinking from was gone. The can has been sent to the Lab to see if the DNA matched that of the earlier found feces. Waters sat back down, and Tate advised him of his rights and continued the questions.

The DA has come in and after getting an update from Captain Carter, he starts pushing for an arrest of Waters. Now, Waters is very upset, and he demands to call his attorney. Tate has no choice but to let him call his lawyer. The DA is demanding that Tate arrest Waters. Tate is asking the DA to hold off until the two DNA samples come back from the feces and the Coke can. But the DA stands fast and will not let up, so Tate makes the arrest and Water's is hauled off. Tate, Captain, and the DA have a meeting in the interrogation room.

"Well guys, great job. Now, when that DNA comes back, that will be the final nail in Waters coffin." the DA said, with an air of confidence and a great deal of arrogance. Tate is not ready to celebrate. He has that crazy feeling that the 'Thin Man' is just not that sloppy. Plus, the search of Waters property came up clean.

"What's up with you Tate? You should be very happy with this. After all, this guy wanted to kill you." The Captain said.

"I hope this is the guy, but I have a bad feeling, the 'Thin Man' is not that dumb."

"Get over it. We got'em and that is all that counts. I don't need another Ramsey type of incident," the DA said, sarcastically. Now they all call it a night and head home. The DA and the Captain are feeling confident and satisfied about the arrest. But Tate is still thinking something was not right.

What no one has talked about are the murders of Doris Dooly and George W. Wilson, and how the missing fingers have started turning up in this case. Only the real 'Thin Man' has this information and now we may never know. Tate was supposed to be off duty for the next few days, but his vacation went up in flames.

8:00 AM, Monday, August 9th, 2007.

Tate is headed back to the office. He's way behind on all those other cases he's working on, but that's the nature of the business. While sitting at his desk going over his E-mails and phone messages. One phone message from Doc. Orwell:

"Tate call me ASAP… I have some bad news for you."

Tate dialed up the Doc, and he picks the phone up on the first ring.

"Orwell, can I help you?"

"Yes, Doc it's Tate, what's up?"

"Tate, you have a big problem, that DNA on the Coke can, does not match that of the poop. So, something is wrong. The DA is going to be very upset if this comes out."

"I tried to tell that crazy power-hungry DA and he just would not give me a break on this one. He's going to give Brad and me a really hard time, and he may try to hide the poop altogether. But now I'm sure that Waters is not the Thin Man."

"What are you going to do?"

"Doc, I hate to say it, but I not only have to try to solve Tony's murder, but I've got Doris Dooly and George W. Wilson's murders to reopen and solve. The thing is, I know who did it. I just don't know the identity of the Thin Man."

"It looks like this Thin Man has been around for a long time, just playing you guys. And Tate, he's not going to be easy to catch. Please be careful, this guy is one in a billion."

"Thanks Doc… just hold off on the DNA thing until I can tell Brad."

Chapter ten

Tate heads over to see Captain Carter with the news and he knows it will get ugly. But when he tells the DA, ugly will look good. After giving Brad the news, Tate listens to him rant, rave and stomp his foot. He even started limping around. Then they just sit quietly for a minute. No one was saying a word. In a minute, Brad burst out in laughter and so did Tate.

"Man, it's time for me to just go on and retire!" Brad said with a smile.

"Brad, I'm sorry, but you know, I was not feeling it when we charged Waters. I even told the DA that we needed to hold off. But, we both know, he will not remember that."

"This, Thin Man is something else. I have never seen anything like this. How many more people has this guy framed? Lord only knows just how many people he's murdered! Tate just get the hell out of here and catch this nut! And Tate, be careful! Keep me up to speed on what the heck's going on."

"Brad, I am going to need some help on this one and I just don't know where to turn. I've been racking my brain, but I keep getting nothing…a big fat NOTHING!"

"Just do your thing, Tate. Just do what you always do, and I'll keep working on the DA." Tate's headed back to his office when he got the idea to call one of his former contacts with the Federal Bureau of Investigations (FBI). Jim Rousch is a Special Agent that has worked profiles on serial killers for over twenty years and he's one of the best in the business. Tate dialed Jim up and they talked for a few minutes. Tate started giving Jim the information on the Thin Man.
After Tate rambles on for a while, Jim softly replied;

"Tate…let me search through my database. This doesn't sound like anyone that I have ever seen or heard about, but you never know. There have been some very high IQ people out there, but none of the people I have seen would match this fellow."

"Have you got any suggestions for me? I need all the help I can get."

"Tate all I can say for now, is please be careful. This killer may have 'Marked' you, and you know how that works."

"Thanks, Jim and let me know what you come up with."

"Okay, Tate have a good day and be careful."

After talking with the FBI agent, Tate called Sally.

"Hey Sally, I need a big favor."

"Well, hello to you Tate. You need to slow down. You're talking to me before I even pick the phone up. Slow down or this case is going to send you over the edge if you're not careful."

"Okay Sally, I know, I know. Look, can you run the phone records for as far back as possible on all the phones for James D. Waters. We just arrested him, but I have a problem with the arrest. I'll e-mail you everything I have on him and it should help you in getting his numbers. Sally, if you could build a database, so we can search for several other numbers that may come up in this case, that would help. I have to go."

"Thank you. Tate, slow down and please be careful."

"Okay Sally, talk soon, I have got to go." Now Captain Carter is at his door.

"Okay, what's up now?" Tate asked.

"The DA needs us in his office…now! He knows about the DNA from the pile of crap." On the way over, Tate is not saying anything, and neither is the Captain. As they walk into the DA's office, they can see that he's not in a good mood.

"You guys are making things too hard. You're trying to mess me up. Now, let's go back over the case. Waters admitted he knew Johnson. He admitted that he had some problems with him at the store. We have video from the McDonald's parking lot that shows him drive up in HIS Corvette, get out, and take the CROWBAR from Ramsey's truck. The McDonald's manager ID'ed HIM as the one that sent you the NOTE to call that phone booth. Plus, we also have a very good photo of him handing the manager the note. HE told you on the phone that, HE KILLED Johnson! So, how much more will a bag of

POOP with someone else's DNA do to this case!!? Also, I have a statement from Joe Applebee, and he has picked Waters out of a photo line-up as the man who paid him to take the call at the phone booth." The DA said in a very angry tone.

"He's a nutty street person that may leave to another town any minute." Captain said, with a sigh. There was nothing the Captain or Tate could say. The DA had made up his mind and he would have to deal with the outcome.

"Yes Sir, we got this." Captain Carter said as they walked out of the DA's office.

"Tate, you need to let this go. If you do anything else with this, you are on your own. I won't be able to help you. But knowing you, I'm just wasting hot air telling you. Because, we both know that you are like a dog with a bone, and nothing I say will stop you."

"Brad, it's not that simple, as I have said before. This Thin Man is still out there, and he's made it personal!"

Tate will be hard charging for the next few

days. Sally has gotten all the phone records ready and Tate has pulled all the files from the Dooly and Wilson cases. It's like a massive jigsaw puzzle with the pieces scattered all over the big office. So far, there has been nothing that connects Waters with Dooly and Wilson. But Tate knows that he needs to prove Waters is out of the equation because Waters, in his mind, is not the suspect.

Chapter eleven

9:34 AM, Thursday, August 12th, 2007:

Tate's phone is ringing, as he sits at his desk working on the massive puzzle. The call is from his FBI buddy.

"Tate, how's it going on that case?"

"It's going, but I have to admit, I'm getting nowhere fast. We have charged a suspect in the case, but I am concerned about it. I think we have the wrong man charged."

"Have you heard anything from the Thin Man?"

"No."

"And you will not hear anything from him until the wrong man has been convicted and another murder has been committed. That's the way he works. He needs the thrill of not only murdering someone and getting away with it, but he likes to make law enforcement look foolish in the process. It's all a part of his sick game. I may have something for you."

"Please, let me have it, anything you have that could help me…I am at my wits end on this."

"Okay, I searched my records and about ten years ago there was a very similar situation in Long Island, New York. The police investigated two different homicide cases. In both cases, the investigators had very good evidence…fingerprints, weapons and other evidence that made it easy to charge and convict the two perpetrators. They even had eyewitnesses in both cases. And guess what? There was one other thing that matches up with your cases."

"Yeah…give it to me man, you have my attention!"

"Tate, each of the victims had one finger removed. And the two men that were charged, were both 6'4" and weighed about 175lbs. These two guys could have passed for brothers."

Then Tate said with a loud voice,

"THIN MAN!! IT'S HIM!!"

"Tate, I hope you get this guy, but it will not be easy. And now all you need to do is just ask, and the FBI will come aid and assist you in anything you need."

"I'll have to run this by the Captain. Then he'll have to run it by the Chief, and so far, the Chief has not been involved. The DA will not want you here because he's tied down on the guy that's been charged." Tate's energy is rising by the minute.

"Jim, can you send me pictures of the two guys that were charged in those cases?"

"Sure, as a matter of fact, I can send you the whole file. After all, the FBI ended up helping in these cases, although we never got anywhere with it."

"Thank you so much. I'll call you back on what the Chief will do. As for me, it would be nice to have y'all take this thing over. But, I don't know how the *brass* will go with that." When Tate hung up the phone, he ran over to Captain Carter's office. Out of breath for a minute, he sat smiling at Brad.

"What in the devil are you so happy about, Tate?"

As he got his breath, Tate told Brad about the call with the FBI agent.

"The DA is going to have your head. It's going to make him look like a fool." Brad said as he rolled his eyes and throw his hands up;

"No! NO! He's the one that made himself look like a fool!" Tate said.

"Tate, the Chief's not going to want the feds around here. He's going to be highly upset about this."

"Brad, I am in too deep, and this Thin Man is just too smart for me. He's already made fools of the Long Island Police and the FBI." Tate knew one thing. The big puzzle he was trying to complete and all the pieces that he'd been swimming around in, was all in vain. All that work was only wasted time because there were no pieces of the puzzle that matched up with the Thin Man. So now, he must move directly to things that would match up with him and him alone, and not all the people that have been unjustly charged thus far. Now, what would connect the Thin Man to the crimes? He knows that he is 6'4", 170 to180lbs, and about forty years old. He has IBS and has been in Long Island NY. He has killed several people and is very, very smart. He also hates law enforcement and he is highly educated. More than likely he is living in Wilmington. It's also a good bet that he carefully selects his victims and the people that he is going to frame. After selecting them, he gets close enough to them that he knows their every move, but not close enough for them to really know him. He then somehow disguises himself to look like the person that he's going to frame or another person that is connected to the victim. It seems that he is very wealthy with no apparent job, or he has a very high paying job that lets him work his own hours.

Chapter twelve

10:17 AM, Monday, August 16, 2007:

Tate receives the material from the FBI and starts going over it. One thing is for sure, there is one eyewitness who has seen the Thin Man face to face. This person identified him as the killer of one victim. Three days later, an innocent person is arrested and pointed out in a lineup, which means that the Thin Man is very good at disguises. He can make himself up to look so much like the people he has marked, that it tricks everyone. He also waited until the second murder suspect was convicted, before he called the police detective and told him that he is the killer. He also gave information that only the true killer would have known to prove that he had done the deed. And now, no one's heard a word from the Thin Man. Tate will get one last call from him just after the DA gets his conviction. This is the biggest part of the game. The Thin Man must let them know just how smart he is and that he is the winner of his sick and demented game.

Tate knows that if he had not stepped in the poop and went to that McDonald's, that Ramsey, and not Waters, would have been going to prison. The Thin Man used Waters as a backup or maybe even a 'patsy' in yet another murder. But, how will Tate force the Thin Man's hand and get him to come out into the open?

9:30 AM, Tuesday, August 17, 2007

Tate is calling the FBI Special Agent.

"Jim, this is Tate. I just wanted you to know that I got those files and I really appreciate it. I really think we can get this guy, but I want to run something by you. The only thing, the pictures of the two guys that could have passed for twins, did not look like Waters. Sure, the size was right, but the faces were not. I want to have that feces that I found analyzed. Do you think that your forensic lab could do that? Maybe, we might find some prescription drugs or something of that nature in it, that could help us ID this guy."

"Look they can pull a lot out of that stuff. But you'll have to get the Chief to make the request. I'll help you any way I can, and you may have something with the poop. It's sure worth a try."

"I know it's a stab in the dark, but I will do anything. Also, I have been looking at schools that teach the art of facial and body disguise. I believe that this guy had to have been disguised as Waters when he went into the McDonald's and he is good at changing his appearance. Now, if we can start connecting the facts. Like finding someone meeting the Thin Man's description, who is or has been enrolled in a theatrical type school. Then, tying in the address history, DNA, and medical information, we might be able to connect the dots."

"Tate, you're on a roll. If the Chief does not let you send that feces sample, call me and I will come down and pick it up. That crap needs to be checked out and one more thing… when our lab examines it, they can tell you just about every drug and chemical that's in it. They can also tell you what the person had to eat for the last few days."

"You know Jim, why the heck do we have to ask the Chief if you can come down?"

"Tate we really don't, due to the fact this case matches up with the Long Island cases. It would be nice if he did ask, but it's just a good political gesture, you know."

"Okay Jim, I'll get back to you ASAP, thanks."

When Tate got off the phone, he called Brad and told him what was going on with the FBI.

"Tate, we have been over this, and you know how the Chief feels about bringing in the FBI. He will have a fit. And you know it."

"Yes, but if he doesn't let them come, they will come in on their own and we can't stop them. This, 'Thin Man' has been killing people in Long Island and they were after him, hot and heavy."

"Yeah, you make a good point, I'll give him the news and you keep me posted on

when they are coming."
After talking with Brad, Tate called Jim at the FBI.

"Jim, how soon can you be here?"

"I'll be there in the morning about 10:30 AM. And Tate, keep that sample on ice. We need to get it to the lab as soon as possible. Oh, and Tate, have everything you've compiled on all three of these cases ready. We will need to build a database. Also, go over everything in your mind about people that have been around you. This guy has been all around you, and you may remember something that may clue you in on him. After all, he did know that you had stepped in his crap behind the store and he told you he knew about your IBS. He is watching every move you make."
When Tate hung up, his mind started racing. He was seeing faces, all types, ages, sizes, races and genders. He was trying to see the same one more than once. He was visualizing all kinds of places, streets, sidewalks, stores, restaurants, and office buildings. He thought of the crime scenes

from the last three murder investigations.
Tate has a very good memory and during this
visualization a few things started to come
back to him… Like the tall black man, about
fifty to sixty years old, short white hair,
sunglasses, big belly, old dirty blue jeans,
and a green long-sleeved shirt. He was
picking up trash on the side of the road as if
he were conducting community service. He
was near Tony's store the day Tony was
killed. He could remember seeing the same
fellow at the McDonalds, as he was going in
with the feces on his shoe. But, what could
this out-of-place, seemingly harmless person
have to do with anything? Tate may never
know, but these thoughts were racing through
his mind. All day and all night, Tate could
not get the suspicious nameless man out of
his mind.

10:20 AM Wednesday, August 18, 2007:

Tate has been sitting at his desk all morning
going over the case files, phone records and
other information regarding the three murder

cases. Now, Jim, from the FBI, taps on the glass to his office door.

"Jim, come on in. Have a seat and tell me what you think about this, 'Thin Man' case."

"We need to get that feces into the lab and you may need to call the investigator with the Long Island Police Department. He may have some information or insight into this case that may not be represented in the reports."

"I sure will, but Jim I did come up with something that was very suspicious. I remembered seeing an old black man on the day Johnson was murdered. It so happens, that I saw him twice that day. Now, it seems very suspicious, and I just can't get 'em out of my mind."

"Tate, I'm going to go on up and talk with Chief Adams. I hope he will come around, because, we are now officially on the case. The FBI will assist you in any way you need. The first thing we're going to do is get the feces sample to the lab." Jim signed the Transfer of Evidence Chain of Custody form and took the sample with him.

About thirty minutes later, Captain Carter called Tate with good news. Chief Adams gave his blessings to work with the Feds. So, Tate's back on the case. So, now he's going to call the investigator in Long Island, to see if they could collaborate and connect a few dots. The phone starts ringing at the office of Detective John King with the Long Island Police.

"Detective King, may I help you?"

"Yes, you can. This is Detective Tate Logan down in Wilmington, NC. FBI Special Agent Jim Rousch told me to give you a call. He thinks that we may have a serial killer that enjoys killing people, cutting their fingers off, and attempting to make the police look foolish."

"Yes, Jim told me to be expecting a call from you. Believe me, I would like nothing more than to catch this monster. But man, it's been ten years and people tend to forget stuff."

"We know this guy is an expert and a master of disguise. And now, with that said, did you ever happen to see, a tall white male... About 6'4" 175 to 180 pounds. Short hair and always dressed in very nice suits. We call him the, 'Thin Man.' He could have been about thirty years old. We think he's about forty now. Also, an old, tall, skinny, black man with short white hair, a pot belly and all dirty looking? Maybe he was around some of the crime scenes? He would have stuck out like a sore thumb."

"Did he have big dark sunglasses, very dirty blue jeans and a dirty green long sleeve shirt on?"

"Heck yeah! Yes! Somehow, these two men are connected." Tate said.

"We thought he was just another vagabond that was just working his area. For the last ten years, I can't get this image out of my mind. I saw him at least five times, in the last murder investigation that I was involved in. This guy that you now call the 'Thin Man.' Humm...I don't recall seeing him myself. The question is, how are we going to find this guy?" The two talked for a few more minutes and Tate asked,

"Did the missing fingers ever turn up in

any of your cases?"

"No, we never saw the fingers, and we never knew why anyone would do such a thing."

"Guess what? Two of the fingers in two of our cases have shown up. One in the Thin Man's' poop, and the other as a print in a phone book. And why he did not get one of Tony Johnson's fingers, we may never know. He called us before we convicted Ramsey. I think the poop shook him up because that's the closest anyone has got to him. And, now that we have Waters charged with Tony's murder, he's gone silent. I suspect he will not make another move until Waters has been convicted."

Detective King tells Tate about the last murder case that he thinks 'Thin Man' was involved in.

"Wait, I remember, the guy that was convicted kept telling us that he stopped into a McDonalds to get something to eat. He got his food and sat down. A clean, well-dressed, tall, white male sat behind him. The man got up, and when he did, he knocked over his drink. Turning over the drink caused a confusion and he thinks the man put something in his drink. The man was so apologetic, that he walked over to the drink fountain machine and got him another drink. But, at the time he thought nothing about it. He did not see him slip anything into his drink, but he really believed it happened. He stated that after leaving McDonald's, as he was driving down the road, he got so sleepy that he had to pull over and go to sleep. The man didn't remember how long he was out. But the next thing he knew, a policeman was removing him from the car and arresting him for murder. He thinks he must have been out for two hours or so."

Tate responded by saying.

"It was as easy as pulling over behind the drugged victim and removing him from the car or just hiding him inside the car. Subsequently, getting into his disguise, driving to the targeted individual, (The Mark) killing him or her and making sure that someone saw him and the car, along with the tag number. Then, driving back and inserting the poor guy back into the driver's seat of his car so the police could find him. A quick call to 911 about a suspicious individual parked on the side of the road."

"Man, this guy is good, and I can see that now, but at the time, no one would have ever believed it."

"You know the tall, well-dressed, white male is the same as the elderly black male. We just don't know who he is." Tate said. After going over a few more details in the different cases, they get back to doing what they do every day, working on all those homicide cases. Tate is really struggling with this case. However, it just seems that the Thin Man can be caught, but how?
The next few days pass without any new results in any of the cases and Tate has been really on edge. All he can think about is the FBI lab and that feces sample that's being analyzed. So, he waits.

Chapter thirteen

10:13 AM, Monday, August 23, 2007:

Tate's phone starts ringing.

"Logan, can I help you?"

"Tate, it's Jim and I have the results from the lab on your sample."

"Okay, give it to me."

"He was eating really good; oysters, pineapple, corn, pecan pie, watermelon, cucumber, green peas, crab, and potatoes. He was also drinking some very expensive wine. They could not tell exactly the year and the vintage. However, if you find the most expensive seafood restaurant in town then you may find the place that serviced the Thin Man. As for the chemicals and the drugs discovered; the drugs that were discovered were some weed, and some Clonazepam, which is an antidepressant."

"Jim... This is going to help in this case. Also, Detective King knows his stuff. We have a connection with a character that

matched up in both of our cases. Now, I
have got to get busy. There is a lot of work
ahead of me for the next few days. Oh, Jim
how in the world do they do that? You
know, figuring out what's in poop?"

"They did tell me a little about that. Ha,
ha, ha. One thing, they found some corn, and
two watermelon seeds in the poop and as for
the crab, the oyster's, wine and potatoes, who
knows."

Tate knows just where to start. The Blue
Crab is the most expensive restaurant in
town. He knows that they have multiple
security cameras in place. So, with a little
luck, he may get another picture of the Thin
Man, only this time he may not be disguised.
Within twenty minutes, Tate is pulling into
the parking lot of The Blue Crab. The timing
is just right 10:45 AM and the Blue Crab is
not yet open. There are several people inside
getting ready to open. Tate gets the attention
of the manager and she lets him in. After
explaining to the manager what he needs.
She takes him into the tape room to look at
tapes. They start rewinding the tapes back to

August 1st. From the 1st to the 3rd would be the days that the Thin Man would have eaten the oysters and crab, along with the wine and other food. As they are looking, Tate tells her why he is looking, and she starts to talk.

"A tall thin man does come in here and he always orders oysters, crab legs, corn and baked potato, and a side of fresh pineapple and fresh watermelon. Oh, he also orders the most expensive wine that we have, I remember because this is such an unusual combination." Then, as a tall man is seen standing at the register getting ready to pay for his meal, the manager said.

"Stop! That's him! That's him!"

"Are you sure?" Tate asked.

"Yes, I'm sure. He's been coming in here for about three or four weeks. He always leaves big tips and he pays with cash every time."

Now, Tate has a very good picture of the 'Thin Man.' He looks nothing like what he was expecting. Okay, Tate now wants to look at the tapes of the parking lot. At the same time, he paid for his meal, the 'Thin

Man' can be seen walking out and getting into a big red RV with a blue top and driving off. Tate was unable to get the tag number, but the RV would be very noticeable. Tate takes all the security tapes and tells the manager to call 911 if they see this guy again, and not to say anything to anyone. Although, he knows how the world works, she's more than likely telling everyone she knows, even before Tate can get back to the station.

Tate is so excited that he nearly falls as he hurries into the station. Captain Carter seeing him stumble, walks over and says;

"Tate, what's going on with you?"

"Brad, we may have this guy. We need to look at these tapes and we need to look at them right now."

"Okay, I'll get the key to the tape room, but Tate, slow down…You're going to have a heart attack."

The rest of the day, Tate searches the tapes looking for more evidence of the Thin Man and the big red RV. He does find a few more images of Thin Man, but no more visuals or glimpses of the RV. Now, Tate is ready to meet with the DA and Brad about their next move.

A meeting is set for 5 PM. with the DA, Captain Carter and himself. Tate has good facial pictures and one good image of the RV. The DA storms into the room.

"Tate! This had better be good! I've had it with you and all this, charge 'em one minute and let 'em go the next minute!"

Up to this point, Tate has not said one single word in any of the meetings with the Captain and the DA. But now he's ready to talk. He slides the pictures across the table to the DA and the Captain. Tate tells them what that worthless pile of crap has done for this case. Tate gave a great overview of how and where they are in this case, and Captain Carter was impressed. The DA now sits, staring at the photos not saying anything. Then he slowly looks up at Tate and said;

"…Tate you along with your FBI friends, have done a good job ID'ing this guy, but you still don't have him yet. So, when are you going to get him?" He then left the room, slamming the door behind him. Captain and Tate started working a plan to get this guy, but even with all they have, they know it will not be easy. A plain clothes unit will set up at The Blue Crab. A picture of the suspect and his RV will be put out to everyone in the department. However, they are not ready to release it to the news, just yet. It would be too easy for the Thin Man to just leave the RV and run with another stolen car. They also know that he wants to hang around until Waters has been convicted. This way he can taunt Tate and law enforcement. Captain Carter will gather all the patrol officers and detectives and they will be on the lookout for the Thin Man and the red RV. There are several RV parks in the city and the surrounding area, so they all will be checked out. One thing about this RV, not only was it red, but it had a dark blue top. It was a very old model Winnebago. So, once again, Tate plays the waiting game. Only this time he is on the road and he's looking everywhere that this RV could possibly be. Tate knows that the Thin Man has not been back to the Blue Crab for about two weeks. Tate realizes he's laying low.

Chapter fourteen

Tate knows that the DA will be forced to clear Waters of all charges, which is the right thing to do. After all, he has not done anything to be held in jail. It is possible he may even bring a lawsuit against the Wilmington Police Department and the City of Wilmington. But Tate wants to talk with Waters before they turn him loose. He had a quick meeting with Brad, and the DA. Afterwards, a meeting was set up with Waters, the DA, Captain Carter and himself. Tate wants to make a deal with Waters.

"Mr. Waters, we have some very good news for you." The DA said.

"What kind of good news?"

"I am going to let Detective Logan tell you what's going on here."

Tate stood up and said, as he looked at Waters and the photo that he had received from McDonald's:

"Mr. Waters we have made a mistake, but I think you can see why we had to bring you in on this murder case. Even you said that this looked just like you and who would know you…better than you? So, with that said, we are dropping all charges on you."

"Yes, you made a big mistake, and you will pay through the nose!"

"Look I understand how you feel. But for one minute can you put yourself in the shoes of two men that are already sitting in prison for committing a murder that they did not commit? Sir…we are dealing with a very smart, but sick individual and we really need to get this guy before he kills again. Do you know just how close you came, to going to prison for a murder that you did not commit?"

The DA stood up and said:

"Mr. Waters, we all here owe Detective Logan a debt of gratitude for working so hard to get the truth in this matter. We all understand just how you must feel about this mistake. But you need to think about the person that really put you in here."

"Mr. Waters, the man behind your face in this photo is the real person to blame…not

Tate or the police department." Brad said as he pushed the photo over to Waters.

"Okay guys I see what's going on and I guess I'll have to let you off the hook on this one." Waters said as he looks at the photo.

"Thank you, Mr. Waters, we really appreciate this. But could we ask one favor of you?" Tate said with a smile.

"What's that? You want a favor from me…?"

"Come on man! You do want to see this crazy man caught. Don't you…?" Tate said.

"Sure, I do. I mean the guy was after me for some reason. First, he stole my car, then he makes people think that he's me, so he can try to frame me for murder. Heck yes, I want to see the guy get caught! But what can I do?"
Now the DA said,

"Right now, he thinks that he's got you, and he will not make a move until you are convicted. Then and only then, will he contact Tate with his sick comments about how stupid he is for convicting the wrong person. And each time he contacts us, we do have a chance to catch him, and that's where you come in. Will you play along with us, by letting people think that you are guilty and even convicted of the crime?"

"How long will this take? And will I have to stay in jail?"

"It will take about two or three weeks and you will not have to stay in jail, but you will have to stay out of sight. Now, can you do this?"

"Okay…okay. I'll play along."
After working out all the details on how they will conduct this plan, Tate takes Waters to a safe place. It's a place that his family can come to see him and a place that he'll be very safe and hidden. Tate and Brad are glad that Waters is not going to be suing anyone. The next day, the evening news reported that, 'Waters would be going to trial in one week, for the first-degree murder of Tony Johnson.' Now, even though, Waters has agreed to go undercover for the police department, by playing along with the DA and this 'mock' trial. No one knows how things will play out. It all may just go up in flames. Only

time will tell.

Chapter fifteen

11:19 AM, Tuesday, August 24, 2007:

One of the patrol officers has found a suspicious red and blue Winnebago. He is told to standby at a safe distance until the SWAT Team and Tate arrived. The location of the Winnebago was off a side road in the woods about two miles outside the city limits. When Tate got the call, his heart started pumping faster with his mind racing. *Have we got him, or has he abandoned the Winnebago and left the country?* All he could think was how much he wanted to cuff this killer. Within a few minutes, everyone arrived and began setting up an action plan. SWAT, armed to the teeth, moved in and surrounded the RV. They knocked the side door in with a battering ram and went inside. But, much to everyone's surprise, the Thin Man was not there, but he had been there. CSI was called in to gather and identify possible evidence. A treasure trove was uncovered. A mask of Waters, and several other masks of people that were unknown to Tate and other investigators in this area was found. Also, there was an assortment of clothing, some new fashionable ones while some were old and dirty. There were several photos of Tony Johnson, Doris Dooly, George Wilson, James Waters and some of Tate. There were many more photos of people that may be victims of the 'Thin Man,' but sorting this out is going to take a lot of time. There was some of the most professional make up kits and liquid plastics and facial transformational products known to man. Now this has allowed Williamston to cast molds of people's faces. So, he could easily disguise himself as if he were those people. There were even some molds of people that no one knew or had any idea of who they were. Lucy's getting some very good fingerprints and the evidence is mounting up fast, but still no Thin Man. The tag number has been run through the DMV and the Winnebago came back to a Thomas H. McLamb of Blue Ridge Road,

Old Falls, N.Y. It had not been reported stolen. An NCIC (Nationwide Crime Information Center) was also run on McLamb and he was clean. He's 84 years old and does not fit the description of the Thin Man. So, why is his RV in North Carolina? A call was placed to Mr. McLamb. A woman, who identified herself as McLamb's wife, told the officers that Mr. McLamb was in a rest home and had been there for over a year. When asked about the Winnebago, she said that as far as she knew, it was still parked on a private lot over near the old fairgrounds. She has not seen it in years.

Tate and the Captain are meeting with the DA and the Chief. They are raising pure hell with Tate and the Captain.

"Tate, why the hell haven't you caught this man!!? Carter, why have you let Tate drag us through the mud!? We look like a bunch of incompetent idiots!" The DA is yelling at the top of his lungs. The Chief is just sitting there, looking at Tate. Captain Carter tries to go to bat for Tate, as he said:

"Listen fellows, you have no idea what kind of homicidal maniac we have here. This guy has eluded police departments and the FBI all over the country. Tate has come closer to getting him than anyone!"
The Chief speaks up.

"It's time we put this guy's picture on the news. We are going to ask for help from the public. We just can't sit on this any longer. Maybe, someone out there can tell us about the Thin Man and that old RV. As for Detective Logan and Captain Carter, they are doing a great job on this case. As a matter of fact, if some 'dumb a' DA had listened to them, two innocent people may have not been charged with a crime that they did not commit. So, we all share some blame here!"
It gets very quiet in the meeting room.

"Okay guys, I get it...I get it...but of the three of us, I'm the only elected official here and at this rate, I'll be out of a job next year."
The DA said.
The meeting ended with the Chief encouraging Tate and Carter to please find this nut. All the Chief could say to the DA

was,

"Don't worry we'll be voting for you, right guys?"

After the meeting, Tate heads to his apartment. He is tired and frustrated. While driving back, he lights up one of those White Owl cigars. It had been a long time and it really felt good. It helps him to calm down and relax. He used to drink whiskey but at times it got him into more trouble than the cigars. He just can't get the Thin Man off his mind. Why did he leave that RV out there? He had to know that it would be found. Why did he leave all that evidence to be found? It's just not like someone as smart as this guy.

Well, it's over tomorrow when his face hits the news on TV. There is no way he sticks around here. As Tate turns off the lamp on his nightstand and rolls over, he knows he's in for a long night. The only light in his room is from the digital alarm clock that sits on his nightstand next to his bed. As he rolls from side to side trying to sleep, the clock tells him that it's 1:00 AM, then 2:00 AM

and now it's 3:30 AM and he's still awake.
He slowly gets out from his bed and sits there
with his head in his hands. All he can see is
the newest face of the Thin Man. Then, he
jumped from the side of his bed, turns the
light on and heads to the bathroom to take a
shower. He stands and lets the water fall
over his body trying to figure out how to
catch the Thin Man. Without even realizing
it, he spent over thirty minutes in the shower.
Now, he knows he will not sleep.
Tate gets out of the shower, gets dressed and
heads out to his car. He's going to the
Waffle House. It's one of his favorite places
for breakfast. It's early, but he's still going.
About five minutes later, he pulls into the
parking lot, gets out, walks in and sits down.
The waiter walks to the table and Tate orders
a cup of coffee, two eggs over medium with
bacon and wheat toast.
In a few minutes as Tate is eating his food,
he spots someone coming into the restaurant
that looks like someone that he's seen before.
Why, what the heck, it's the tall black man
with that pot belly, dirty jeans and all. At

about the same time, the subject spots Tate. As Tate is rushing towards the man, the suspect is making a break across the parking lot. Now, both these fellows are not young, and they are not in the best shape. Both are running like they are young again. Tate is yelling,

"Stop! Police! Stop!" But the subject is not slowing down. They run out of the parking lot and down the street. They go around a shopping mall and down a dark alley. Although Tate isn't gaining any ground, he keeps running. Now, the man approaches a door that leads to a flight of steps. As he gets near the top of the steps, Tate's now quickly gaining on him. The man goes into a room at the top of the steps. As the door slams shut, Tate gets there, but the door has been locked. Tate yells;

"Open the door, you are under arrest! Give it up! Backup is on the way." But backup is not on the way, because Tate's police radio is back in his apartment and his cell phone has fallen from his pocket while chasing the suspect. Tate is on his own with a cold-blooded killer. Fortunately, Tate does have his nine-millimeter pistol. Now, you could hear a pin drop. Tate kicks the door as hard as possible, but the door doesn't budge.

"Open this door! Open this door!" As Tate got a breath to yell once more, he could hear the man softly say...

"You win… you were the best one, Mr. Logan, you got me, yes you did."
Now, the doorknob slowly turns, and the door starts to open. Tate gives a big push on the door and knocked the man to the floor. Tate kept his weapon pointed at the man while giving him orders to keep his hands over his head while lying on the floor. The whole time this is going on the man is laughing almost uncontrollably.

"Ha ha ha ha! I don't have a weapon on me, but I know you will have to search me to make sure. Don't be extemporaneous in your duty. Ha ha ha ha!"

"I will kill you if you make any foolish moves. You are under arrest! I am charging you with the murder of Tony Johnson! You have the right to remain silent, anything you say can be used against you in a court of law. You have the right to have an attorney present. If you cannot afford an attorney, one will be appointed to represent you. Do you understand your rights?"

"Yes Sir. Mr. Logan, I understand. You have run into a trap. You will never take me in, and I've got you! Ha! Ha! Ha! Ha!" The man sarcastically and dramatically said. Now as Tate was standing there with the Thin Man taunting him, everything suddenly and unexpectedly went black. Tate lay on the cold, nasty hard floor for the rest of the night, while the Thin Man slips off into the night to parts unknown.

Chapter sixteen

7:32 AM, Wednesday, August 25, 2007:

Now the sun is shining, and a glimmer of light peeks through the dirty windows. Tate is beginning to wake up. As his eyes slowly open, everything is a blur and Tate's head is hurting, and hurting extremely badly. He has a goose egg on the top of his head that is pounding away. For about an hour, Tate is going in and out of consciousness. As he starts to come around, he knows that at least, his heart is beating. He can feel every beat in the top of his head.

"That son of a gun has got me again." As he slowly gets up from the floor, he can see a large cinder block tied to a rope that had been hanging over the door and is now on the floor with a chunk of his hair on the side of it. As Tate slowly leaves the area, he's thinking; *This guy is just too smart, and I can't believe that I still have all my fingers. And why didn't he just kill me? But then he wouldn't have someone to play this crazy game with.*

Tate's making his way back to his car in the parking lot at the Waffle House, when he finds his cell phone in the grass next to the sidewalk. As he picks it up, he dials Captain Carter. Carter can see that it's Tate calling him.

"Tate! Where are you? You are late for work!"

"I know Brad, I know, I overslept. But I'm on the way in now."

"Just get in here as fast as you can. The DA is missing, and his wife is going bonkers! He went out last night at about nine and did not go back home. So, we've got a big problem!"

Tate needed a shower and some clean clothes. No time for that now. He heads on down to see Captain Carter. Shortly Tate arrived and walked into Brad's office.

"Tate, where the hell have you been? You look like you spent the night inside a dumpster. What's going on with you and why are you so dirty?"

Tate explains to Brad what happened to him, and now Brad wants Tate to go to the hospital to be checked out. But Tate is not having that.

"Brad, tell me about the DA…what's going on?"

"He's missing, and no one knows anything. But you know, with what happened to you, I've got a very good idea that the Thin Man has got his hand in this. And, I told you, to be careful! How could you let him get the drop on you!?"

Tate just could not find the words for Brad. He just rubbed his aching head and looked down at the floor. Brad told him to go home and get cleaned up and get back to work or go to the hospital. Tate goes back to his apartment, gets a shower and some clean clothes, then heads back to the station to help look for the DA.

On the way back, he's looking at everything and everybody, something suspicious or out of place. He still can't get over how he let the Thin Man get the jump on him and why the Thin Man has marked him. One thing for sure, the meeting last night was not by accident. The Thin Man has been waiting for the opportunity of a chance meeting for some time. So, how is it that the Thin Man can keep surveillance on a seasoned police officer, without being burned? Tate had not seen any suspicious vehicles sitting around and he had not seen any cameras in 'out of the way' spots. He had checked his vehicle for any hidden tracking devices. He found nothing. As Tate pulls into the parking lot at the police station, he can see Brad going into the station and he's not looking happy, not happy at all. As if Tate's head wasn't already hurting enough, he's got a feeling it's not going to get any better. Tate needs to get to Brad before he gets to his office. It would be much better talking with Brad in private. So, Tate jumps out and runs to catch up before he gets to the office. As Tate gets to the elevator, he can see Brad standing there waiting. Just as the door opens Tate grabs Brad on the arm;

"Brad, can I talk with you?"

"Sure Tate, come on up, I need to talk to

you anyway."

"No Brad, I need to talk to you in private."

"Okay, Tate." As they step back from the elevator, they turn and walk into an empty conference room and close the door.

"Okay Tate, this had better be good. Now, what is it?"

"Brad, you know the Thin Man's got the DA. He's either killed him or knocked him out like he did me last night, but he's got'em."

"That's good Tate, that's really, good! We know the Thin Man is behind this, but that's all we know."

"Brad, he could have killed me last night, but he didn't. It's a game with this guy and he's marked me as his main prize. Now, he may not kill the DA, but he will use him as a part of his sick game. He will contact me about the DA. I am pretty sure that I know how and when, and when he does, the DA will only have a short time to live. It will be up to me, to find where the DA is being kept and I'll only have a short time to do it."

"Tate what makes you think you know how

and when? Have you started reading minds?"

"No, But, if I am right, that pay phone will be ringing today at 5:00 PM, on the dot."

"You're right! You're right, he will. But this time keep 'em on long enough. I'll get everything set up and we'll try again."

"Brad, I sure hope I'm right about this and we can find the DA before it's too late. If the Thin Man's keeping the score, it's Thin Man, 5 and Tate 0. So, somehow, I would like to get one point on the board."

All day long, every law enforcement officer in the city and county were looking for the missing DA. They were not finding him or anything that would suggest his whereabouts. Tate has been dealing with a bad headache as he desperately connected the dots. His mind kept going back to the dirty room where the Thin Man led him before making a fool out of him.

And that laugh, that the Thin Man let out was so strange. He's heard that laugh before and for the life of him, he can't place it. That laugh just keeps replaying in Tate's mind.

Chapter seventeen

4:50 PM:

Everyone has been in place for several
minutes. Tate's standing by at the pay phone
and the Captain has set everything up once
more, in hope of getting a fix on the Thin
Man.

5:00 PM:

Nothing. The phone is not ringing. Tate has a
very bad feeling and the Captain is worried
that Tate is about to make them all look bad.

5:10 PM:

The phone is still not ringing.
    "Okay Tate, it was a good thought, but it's
not going to happen. I'm sorry but I'm going
to pull the team off."
    "I'm sorry Brad. I'll see you in the
morning."

Tate just sits there looking at that phone booth, with a sinking feeling that he's let the team down and wondering what went wrong. With everyone else gone, he decides to leave. Now the phone starts to ring. Tate jumped out of his car and ran up and answered the it. The first thing Tate heard was that laugh.

"Ha Ha Ha Ha Ha, Mr. Logan, you're the dumbest person that I've ever met. But I've got to hand it to you. You knew how I would make contact, so I'll give you a point for that! Ha Ha Ha Ha!! Oh, by the way, how's your head? Ha Ha Ha!"

"Look you sicko, what did you do with the DA?!!"

"Oh, he's a little tied up now, but I'll have him call you later."

"Okay, what do I need to do!?"

"You need to think! Think man! Think! Someone with such a small worthless brain would have a very difficult time thinking. You know, you've got three hours and not a minute more to come up with where the DA (Dumb A.) is located. And if you find him, he's all yours. If not, he's mine. Well, maybe not all of him. I'll keep one of his fingers for old time sake. Tate, your time started at 5:00 p.m. today."

Click. Once more the time ran out or maybe not. *Did the tech guys stay on or did they lose the call again?* Tate is thinking as he called Captain Carter with the news.

"Brad! He called! I sure hope the guys were able to trace the call."

"No Tate, the team pulled off when I did, so once again, no trace."

"Brad, we got two hours and forty-eight minutes to find the DA and if not, the Thin Man will kill him and cut one of his fingers off. One more thing Brad…is there a carnival in town?"

"I think there is. Why do you ask?"

"Never mind, it is at the old fairgrounds, right!"

"Yes, that's where it always is every year about this time. Why do you ask?"

"Never mind, you would not believe me if I told you anyway." Tate said as he quickly disconnected, leaving Brad with a big question about why Tate's asking about the carnival.

5:46 PM:

Tate drives by the old fairgrounds. The carnival has been in town for over a week and Tate knows that the DA is in there somewhere. He's thinking and he's thinking hard. To beat the Thin Man, he must start thinking as the Thin Man would. He quickly surveys the area and then speeds away before anyone can see or recognize him.

6:11 PM:

Tate is pulling into the driveway to an old friend's house. Chuck Barnes is a retired police officer and he's also a Shriner. Every year when the Shriner's have their parade, Chuck dresses as a clown and hands out candy and makes balloons for the children. Tate's in luck, as he pulls into the driveway, he can see Chuck in the front yard. Tate gets out and greets Chuck.

"Chuck, how're things going?"

"Great, and what brings you to my place?"

"Chuck, I have an unusual request."

"Tate, now what could that be?"

"Chuck, I need to borrow your clown suit. I sure hope you'll help me out. It's a life and death situation. Chuck, I don't have time to explain it, but if you could help, it would mean the world to me."

"Sure, but if you are going to wear it, I'll have to do the clown makeup for you."

"Can we do it right now?"

"Sure, come in and I'll fix you right up."

6:50 PM:

Chuck has Tate looking good. Tate's a happy clown. He still hasn't told Chuck anything about why he needs the suit, just that it's a life and death matter. Chuck puts the final touch on Tate including the big red nose. Tate jumps into his car and heads back toward the carnival.

7:11 PM:

Time is running out for the DA as Tate
arrives. He parks in the rear parking lot
where he noticed a large hole in the fence.
He eased out of his car and crawled through
the hole and into the busy activities of the
carnival. Tate had been told about the hole in
the fence by the owner a few weeks ago.
The owner had also been asked to fix the
hole, but Tate knew that the owner was
unlikely to repair the fence. He's just too
cheap to spend money that will not profit
him.
The carnival is going strong, with a big
crowd of people walking about and enjoying
the festivities. The smell of hot dogs, funnel
cake and other good smelling things are
heavy in the air. The noise from the crowd
and the carnival music was blasting away in
Tate's ears. It's surreal how the carnival
never changes. Even that music; Dut dut
dutely dut, do do do dut dudly do, and so on
just like it was when Tate was a kid. He is
walking about acting like a clown and

looking for other clowns. People are looking and laughing at Tate, but no one knows who he is. Tate even spots a few people that he knows. It seems funny to Tate that they have no idea that it's him in the clown suit. In a strange way, Tate is beginning to see how the Thin Man must feel when he is in disguise. Tate heads to the motorhomes and travel trailers that are parked to the side of the main area of the runway. There are not many people in this area…only an occasional carnival worker moving from one side to the other as they go back into the main area. Suddenly, Tate observed a fellow clown go into an old RV. The clown had the sad, Emmett Kelly look. (Emmett Kelly was a very famous clown in the 50's and 60's). Just as he steps inside the RV, the sad clown lets out that laugh… and now Tate's sure that this is the Thin Man. Tate works his way closer and closer to the RV. Tate must be very careful. He just needs to act like he's supposed to be here like everyone else. Maybe, he's a new clown that just joined the carnival. Who would know?

Now at last, Tate has worked his way to the rear of the RV. He can see a small window on the side of the RV. The curtain on the window is open enough, that if Tate could get up high enough, he could see inside the RV. He looks down and spots a wooden crate that he could step on that would get him up enough to see inside the RV. He very quietly moves the crate over to the window. As he's doing this the side door on the other side of the RV slams shut. This startles Tate, causing him to drop to the ground to hide. After a minute, the coast is clear, so Tate stands up and steps up onto the wooden crate. As he looks in the RV, he can see the DA is all tied up with duct-tape over his mouth. He's sitting in a chair in the middle of the floor of the RV. He is alive but appears to be unconscious. A small table is positioned in front of the DA. On the table were a pair of rubber gloves, a plastic sandwich bag, a set of pruning shears, and an icepick. The only good thing about this is the DA seems to still have all his fingers intact.

Tate wants to call for help, but he wants to

wait until the Thin Man returns to the RV. However, the DA's safety is at stake and Tate can't gamble on this, so he makes the call. Tate calls Captain Carter on his cell phone.

"Brad I found the DA and the Thin Man. They are at this traveling carnival at the old fairgrounds. The DA's tied up inside one of the RV's that's parked behind the main strip. I am behind the RV and the Thin Man is on the grounds, but I don't know where right now. He's dressed in a clown suit."

"Tate, I'll get the team together and get out there as soon as we can."

"No! Brad just come on out, we are about to run out of time! It's eight minutes to eight."

"I'm on the way. Please be careful, this guy has an advantage over you. You are in his world now."

"Brad, Brad! He's the sad clown and I'm the happy one!"

"What? Tate, what are you talking about?" (But Tate hung up before explaining it to Brad). Now, all Tate can do is wait for the

Thin Man to go back into the RV. He only has a few more minutes.

7:56 PM:

Tate can hear that laugh getting closer and closer to the RV. Ha, Ha, Ha, Ha… (Tate's thinking: *The usual sad clowns never laugh or talk, so why's this guy laughing in a Sad Clown suit? This guy is a strange bird.*) Tate can see the side door open from the window on the back side. The Thin Man cautiously enters the RV and he slowly closed the door behind him. Tate moves quickly to the side door that the Thin Man just entered through. As Tate slowly opens the door, he can see the Thin Man standing by the DA, with his back to him.

"Well…now, Mr. DA… Apparently, no one will be coming to save you. How unfortunate." Thin Man said as he rips the tape from the DA's mouth.

The DA is coming out of an unconscious state. He struggles with confusion and with an exhausted and dazed look on his face. He starts to beg the Thin Man for compassion. He's pleading for his life. But the Thin Man just starts to do his thing, as he puts the rubber gloves on and reaches for the icepick. He starts that crazy laugh. Tate knows he's got to make his move, and he's got to move fast. As he pulls his weapon, he yells…

"Drop that icepick and turn around with your hands up! You are under arrest!" At this time, the Thin Man slowly turns around, he drops the icepick.

"Tate… you have completely and extremely surprised me, you're maybe a little smarter than I thought." Now, facing Tate, all he could say was:

"How…? How did you…?"

"Get on the floor and this time, no booby traps and no laugh!" Thin Man knew, Tate had the upper hand and escaping was not likely. In the background, they could hear the sirens wailing away, getting closer and closer.

Tate very cautiously cuffed Thin Man and approached the DA, getting him loose from the duct tape. The DA is so emotional that he's crying and thanking Tate with all his might. Captain Carter and several police officers arrive at the RV. Carter takes one look at Tate and burst out with a laugh.

"Tate! Is that you?! I think I've seen it all now! How in the world did you end up in that get- up and how in the world did you get the Thin Man?!"

"Brad, it wasn't easy. This nut has turned us all every which way but loose. But it was that crazy laugh that he let out the first time I arrested him. You know, just before he knocked me out with that cinder block, I knew that I had heard that laugh. But I just couldn't think of where. Right after I talked to him on the pay phone today, it hit me. Two years ago, about this time of the year, Tony and I were killing a little time and decided to come over to the carnival. Well, while here I remember this nutty clown, sure it was just another clown, but he was so weird. When he laughed it sounded so crazy, even Tony commented about it. So, I decided to use my own disguise, the clown suit. I knew that no one, not even this nut would know who I

was. As it turned out, I just got lucky. I saw
him go into the RV, and when he did, he let
out with that crazy laugh. Now, I was sure it
was our man. Brad, it was just plain luck.
That's all!"
Captain Carter said with a laugh of his own.
"Ha ha ha. Tate, luck or no luck, you have
saved the DA and this guy will be off the
street. I know the Feds and the Long Island
Police will be anxious to get their hands on
him. There is no telling how many people
he's killed. The people that he's framed will
really be glad he's been caught."
Tate and Brad took the Thin Man to the
police station to be booked and questioned,
while two police officers stayed back to
protect the crime scene until CSI arrived.
The DA was taken to the hospital by EMS.

Chapter eighteen

Back at the station, the Thin Man was fingerprinted and processed. Also, a DNA sample was obtained and taken to the lab for analysis. The Thin Man was read his rights once more, but for some reason, he became very quiet. He still would not give his real name. He just would not tell them anything at all. He was in the interrogation room all alone. Tate and the Captain are looking at him through the one-way glass and the Thin Man knows. Only now, they are seeing the real Thin Man, because all the makeup from the clown mask has been washed away. He's a white male, short dark hair, blue eyes, with a dark complexion.

"Tate, you get out of your clown suit and get cleaned up and I'll start the questioning."

"Okay Brad, I'll be glad to get out of this makeup and get back to my old self." Tate said as he heads off to the locker room to get cleaned up.

At this point, Captain Carter walked into the

interrogation room. He pulls a chair back from the table and slowly sits down across from the Thin Man. They just look at each other for a few seconds.

Captain Carter said;

"You know that we got the goods on you. You've lost this silly game and Tate has beaten you up pretty good. He's caught you and you know it. Now, you can make it easy, or you can make it hard on yourself, it's up to you."

The Thin Man just looks at Carter, smiles and replies:

"I've got to admit it, Tate's much smarter than I gave him credit. Yes, who would have thought that he would have got me with my own laugh? It has been two years."

"I'm glad you've admitted that he's got you. The kidnapping of the DA and the murder of Tony Johnson is going to put you on death row. So, why don't you tell us all about how you have put several people in prison for what you've done. And how you've made fools of law enforcement, not to mention the FBI? A confession could keep you off death row, and you'll still get credit for being one of the smartest serial killers in modern history. Yes, people will be talking about you a hundred years or longer."

"Detective Carter, do you think I'm really that stupid? Do you really think I'd fall for that?"

"No, I'm not saying that I think you are stupid. No. No way I'd say anything of the sort. We all know how smart you are. Tate admitted that it was just dumb luck that he found you at the RV. If you don't bring everything that you've done out into the open, no one will ever know about what you've done and how you were able to pull it off."

Now, Tate's back at the window and he's all cleaned up and ready to get into that room with his nemesis. As he looks through the one-way glass, the Thin Man looks up, right at him as though he can see through the glass. Tate is thinking, *this guy knows that I am standing right here and he's still playing with me.* So, Tate walks into the room where Brad and the Thin Man are. As Tate walked into the room, Thin Man looks at him and says; "Officer Logan, it looks like you are a winner after all. You are the Man! Yes, Sir! You are the man!"

"Look, I was just doing my job the best I could. Now, why can't you give us your name? You know that we'll get it sooner or later." Tate said with a very humble voice. Captain Carter, studied for a minute and said:

"You know, we've been calling you the 'Thin Man' for a long time now. So just give us your name. If not, then we'll have to start calling you 'John Doe' and we don't like calling people John Doe."

They want to get him to start talking. They will pull every trick they have, to get him going, but he will not be easy. At this point, there is very little known about him, and they got that from the carnival boss. He told a police officer that the sad clown, also known as, Bill Clancy, has been working with the carnival for ten years and they travel up and down the east coast. He first got on with them while they were doing the carnival in Long Island, New York. They don't know where he's from and they really don't care. When he joined the carnival, he seemed to have a lot of money. He never complained about making low wages because he enjoyed the lifestyle. He was a loner that stayed to himself and no one was ever able to get close to him. Now, Tate starts asking the obvious question.

"Okay, Bill Clancy? That is your name? Right! How long have you been working with the carnival?"

"If that's what you want to call me, that's good. Some people have been calling me that for years. And, yes… I have been traveling with the carnival for ten years and I do like to stay to myself. I have a hard time making friends. All except you, Tate. We have bonded like brothers, now haven't we?" Tate nor the Captain said a word. They just looked at Bill, or John Doe or Thin Man or whatever his name might be.

"You are really good, Officer Logan. I will talk, but only to you. Until the good Captain leaves the room, I will not say another word." Tate looks at Brad, and Brad gets up and walks out of the room.

"Okay, the floor is all yours, now tell me about yourself."

"Sure thing, but you better make sure that tape recorder has fresh batteries because it's going to take a while."

Tate's feeling good about this, but he knows this guy can't be trusted.

Now, for no reason, the Thin Man goes all the way back to his childhood.

"I lived in a big house as an only child. My father was a self-made millionaire and my mother was a Southern Belle that loved to show off. Her mother and father died in a house fire when she was a little girl. Her aunt raised her until she left home at the age of eighteen. So, I never remember anyone on my mother's side of the family. My grandmother on my father's side died before I was able to meet her. I did get to meet and know my grandfather on my father's side. I never knew he existed until I was nine years old. No one ever talked about them, not a word…" Then, a slight pause before continuing.

"My father was always out of town making money and my mother just could not stand to be around him. I went to a private school with a bunch of other rich kids whom I hated, and they did not like me either. I did have one good friend. That friend was one of the people that worked for my father around the house. He was like the Butler, the handyman, the whatever needed to be done man. He really looked after my mother, especially when dad was out of town."

He then stopped for a minute. A strange look on his face begun to emerge. His eyes...it was something about his eyes. Suddenly, he looked at Tate and started back with his story once more. This time he refers to himself as if someone else is telling the story.

"One day, the little fellow came home early from school and caught them in her bedroom. He was only nine years old and what he saw really bothered him. They knew that he had seen them, and they wanted to keep him from telling his dad. They told him that what they were doing was just a game. It was just a game, and no one should ever know. It would be their little secret and no one would ever tell anyone about what he had seen.

"So, to make this seem right and good they made him a part of the game. They would come up with a different game every week. They would have clues that would be hidden all over the house. After a while, he forgot about what he had seen between the handyman and his mother.

"I must admit it could have been fun for the little fellow or it could have been pure hell for him. But as quickly as it started…it ended."

The Thin Man stopped for a minute, as though, he was trying to process what he wanted to say next. Now he takes off once more, while Tate kept very quiet.

"One day, they come in with… you guessed it, a clown suit, no not just one but two clown suits. One has a happy face and one had a sad face. Both these suits fit the little fellow and only him, and to start with his mother would put the face paint on, but later he learned how. He just kept getting better and better over the years. The deal was if he was able to win the game, he was able to put the happy clown suit on and they would have a big party with just the three of them. If he could not get all the clues and he lost the game, he would have to put that sad clown suit on and play another sick game with his mother and the handyman. This game was no fun, no fun at all, for the little fellow. They made him watch as they played their sick games in bed. The day his father came in and caught them in the bedroom, that was bad... They were doing their sick thing and the little fellow was watching. His father went off the deep end and killed his mother and the handyman. For some reason, he cut the handy man's right index finger off. He also cut his wife's right pinky finger off. Why he did this no one will ever know. Afterwards, he beat the little fellow almost to death. The little boy was found alive that day, but he stayed in the hospital for two months. When he got out of the hospital his old estranged grandfather on his father's side was there to pick him up. He found out from him that his father had killed himself the same day that everything went down. He never got over that and I guess that's what made Sad Clown what he is today."

Tate just sat and listened to the Thin Man. Not saying or doing anything that would stop him from talking. One thing Tate learned years ago, was never stop the suspect when they are talking. It's hard enough to get them to talk, so when they start, let them keep going. The only thing about this confession was the way it was being told.

Now, the Thin Man has once again stopped for a minute. So, Tate softly asked:

"So, will you tell me what your real name is?"

"My real name… You know, I have not used that name in many years, and I have tried to forget it. But it's, Reginald Albert Williamston III. I was born in, Richmond, Virginia and I am forty-one years old. My address is where I am at the time. I have millions of dollars that I can tap into anytime I want. I usually get a large amount of cash from my account about two times a year. I don't own a car or even the RV's that I've been driving around."

Tate asked;

"What would you like us to call you from here on?"

"I don't care, I was really getting used to the Thin Man, but you can call me Bill Clancy if you like."

"Okay Bill, we can go with that, for now. But at some point, we are going to have to use your given name." Captain Carter has been patiently monitoring the interrogation. He's very satisfied with Tate. After all, Tate's one of the best at getting criminals to talk. Now, the Thin Man or as he will be known for now as Bill Clancy, was beginning to talk once more.

"Mr. Logan, I'm going to tell you everything that I've ever done, but you are going to have to promise me one thing."

"…I'll try, but before I can promise, I'll need to know what you're asking?"

"It's hard for me. I know that you're not going to want to do this, and it really sounds kind of stupid. But if you don't do it, I am going to clam up. And if I clam up you will never know what I have to say. And believe me, what I've got to say will be big, big... You have no idea just how big."

Tate wants to tell him yes, but he has no idea what it means. Because if he says no, it's over. If he says yes, it's no telling what this guy will want. So, Tate looks at a spot on the one-way glass in the direction of Captain Carter. Now, Tate has his radio on with his earpiece in. He and Brad have their signals. If Brad hit's the mike button two times, it's no, if he hits it three times, it's yes. Tate waits and Brad presses the button three times. Giving him a yes.

Tate looks at Bill for a few seconds:

"Okay, but if it's unreasonable, the brass around here will stop me. But you have my word, yes. So, what do you want?"

"You know, I have worn that sad clown suit for so long, doing so many terrible things. Now, that I want to get all the terrible deadly deeds off my chest. I need to have my happy clown suit on. That's all I want! I promise, if I can put that thing on and get the good side of me out into the open, you will be told everything that the Sad Clown has ever done!"

Tate gets up and tells Bill that he'll be right back. He walked out, and Brad meets him at the door.

"Brad that outfit is in that RV. Can you get someone from CIS to bring it over here?"

"Yes, Tate, it's on the way. You are doing great. Keep him going… there's no telling what he's going to confess."

Tate stepped back into the room with a tray of paper cups, ice, some water and drinks. He sits it on the table and asks Bill what he wanted. Bill asked for a regular coke with ice. Tate opened a Coke and poured it for Bill. At this time Tate loosened the cuffs, so Bill could drink the Coke.

Chapter nineteen

The Happy Clown outfit is on the way.
Within a few minutes, Brad walked into the
room with the Happy Clown makeup and
suit. Then, with some of the police custody
officers observing, Bill Clancy comes to life
as the Happy Clown. The officers left the
room and Tate walked in and took a seat
across from Bill or as he's now called,
'Happy Clown.' It was like talking to a nine-
year-old child. What he would say was one
for the books. He talked and gave great
details of ninety-eight different murders that
the Sad Clown had committed. He had been
killing all over the east coast for more than
ten years! This went on all night long.
Neither Tate nor the Happy Clown weakened
or tired. Tate felt an energy that he had not
felt in quite some time.
The Happy Clown also revealed why the Sad
Clown hated and reviled the police so much.
As it turns out, one of the costumes that his
mother's lover would wear, was a police

uniform. And those fingers… well I think you know about that. That was the last thing the little boy, or at this point the Sad Clown, would see the day his father nearly beat him to death. One thing that we'll never know is why and which one of the different personalities ate the finger. But there was much more that was not told.

Tate sat and listened to Happy Clown until the wee hours of the morning, learning about all the murders that Sad Clown had committed. This whole thing was so astonishing. Tate just had to ask Happy Clown;

"Why did Sad Clown pick Tony and the others? Why did he want to frame those innocent people?"

"While working and traveling with the carnival, we got to go all over the east coast. It was up to him how long or how much he worked. We moved about freely. We have been in this town many times. After all, the carnival comes to town every year at about the same time. We remembered reading about you in the newspaper. All those murder cases that you solved, really impressed us. As for Tony, he was your best friend so that marked him. As for Ramsey, Sad Clown knew that he was parking in the woods almost every day, so he just happened to be in the wrong place at the wrong time. As for Waters, he's another fellow that looks like and reminds Sad Clown of dear old dad. That arrogant SOB! Sad Clown wanted to set him up. He would have too, if not for you! But what got us, was that pile of crap Sad Clown dropped behind the store." Williamston said with vile hatred fuming from his eyes, as if the Sad Clown was trying to come out.

"What you didn't know about, was the old black gentleman that you saw picking up the trash in the road that day…well, he was standing by that big sign next to Tony's on the side of the road. He was watching you, as you scooped the crap into the evidence bag. That really got to him. Who would think of such a thing? He also knew that there was a good chance that Doris' finger was in that stuff. How it got there? I'll never know. But that was big!

"Now, the old black gentleman...Sad Clown created him to resemble the man that was having the affair with our mother. He worked on him for years. As a matter of fact, I think that he may have even aged him a little as time went on. To us, that kept him more realistic. Doris Dooly was one that reminded us of our mother. He kept a check on her for four years. George Wilson, well, Sad Clown just did not like his looks. We didn't know him like the rest. He too just happened to be in the wrong place at the wrong time. As for those fools that you sent to prison for murdering Dooly and Wilson... just easy marks, very easy.

Now, they will get, a 'get out of jail free card.' Man! Sad Clown hates that! Oh, and by the way, Sad Clown was planning to send you Tony's right index finger, but someone come up before he could get it. About the big red and blue RV, that was just one of several RV's that we borrowed over the years. And, the day that the officer discovered it, we were in the woods because of the IBS. Man, we could not believe he spotted that thing. It was two miles outside the city limits. Lucky for us that we had another RV and another mask of the old black gentleman."

Tate had to ask.

"Okay, Mr. Happy Clown... What was going on the night you led me into that trap?"

"Ha, Ha, Sad Clown had been waiting for you to go into the Waffle House for several days. He knew you were not sleeping, and he figured that one morning very early, you would come on down. And, just as he had calculated, there you were. Then, he stumbled in as the old black man, and allowed you to see him."

"But, why didn't he kill me and cut one of my fingers off? You know, he had me."

"But Tate... Tate... The game would have been over, and Sad Clown would have had to find another poor fool to torment. Besides, he has never killed a police officer, that would be a very bad thing to do."

All night, Tate patiently listened, and he did ask a lot of questions. Tate asked

Williamston how he was able to change from one disguise to another so fast. Williamston would just look at Tate and say, nothing, nothing at all. This was getting to Tate, but he did not want Williamston to know. So, he never pushed the issue. After all, that was not a big deal at this point.

As the sun was coming up, the questions stopped, and Happy Clown was cleaned up and taken to a jail cell. Tate, Brad and some of the other officer's that had been up all night, headed home to get some rest.

It was a very long night and one that Tate would never forget if he lived to be a hundred. There were many questions that were not answered. They may never be. But Williamston will be questioned once more in a couple of days by the FBI. They will be looking much deeper into the murderous and mysterious past of Mr. Williamston. Brad and Tate did manage to get some well-needed rest, but soon it's back to work, and there will be a lot to get done. The FBI will be coming to question Williamston concerning all the murders that he has

confessed to committing up and down the
east coast.

Chapter twenty

9:17 AM, Thursday, August 26, 2007:

Tate and Captain Carter meet with two FBI Agents at the police station. Special Agent, William McCarthy and Special Agent Nathan Wilkins, have been sent to question Reginald Albert Williamston III, AKA Bill Clancy, AKA Sad Clown/Happy Clown. They have several very large boxes of files, that contains ninety-eight murder cases that are more than likely connected with Williamston.   And they are eager to start working. But first they must go over the taped confession that Williamston gave Tate. This will take three to four days. Then they must set up a line of questions on each case, to find out the true facts surrounding each case.

This will be a major job. When the confessions were given to Tate, they were given with amazing detail in each case. They included the times, the victims, the police, the witnesses and locations along with the murder weapons and the names of the people who were framed. Williamston has a photographic memory and an eye for the slightest detail. Some of the tricks that he used on the 'marks' were extremely brilliant. Before he would shoot someone with a gun that the 'marked' perpetrator owned, he would place the gun in the unconscious person's hand and fire it off. That way the gunpowder residue would be on their hand. He would then reload the gun while using gloves and then later shoot the unsuspecting victim…the 'mark' that was set to be murdered. He was an expert marksman; in every case he killed the victim with only one shot. When he would return the 'marked' perpetrator, back to their vehicle, he would leave the murder weapon in their hand, thus sealing the case against them. In the cases where he killed people without an eyewitness, he used an ice pick. He would often taunt them for hours before finally killing them by sticking it into the left ear.

In some cases, such as in the case of Tony Johnson, he would use something like a crowbar that belonged to the person that he 'marked' as the murderer. It would have their fingerprints all over it. It's hard enough to believe that Williamston was able to get away with just one set up. But, to commit as many as he did, was completely out of the realm of belief.

9:31 AM, Wednesday, September 8, 2007:

For two weeks, the FBI agents had been going over the confession and the files of all the different murders that had been committed. Now, they are ready to question the suspect. On the morning they are set to start their interview with Williamston, they have a meeting with Tate and Captain Carter. The meeting is opened with a complicated flow chart that has been created using the confession and the files of each murder. It is, to say the least, a very sophisticated and professional presentation. Everyone is really feeling good at this point.

Although they have the confession, they want to talk with Williamston to see what more they can get. The meeting did not last very long, and Williamston was placed in the interrogation room for questioning by the FBI. They all stand at the one-way glass watching while Williamston sat alone in the room. At one point, Williamston looked up at the glass and looked at each person just like he could see them. He knew they were looking at him.

Tate went into the room alone and sat down in front of him. As they were sitting there, Tate asked:

"So, how's things going? Have they been treating you well?"

"Why…Mr. Logan, how are you today?"

"I'm good, and I hope you are."

"Now, Mr. Logan, what can I do for you today?"

"I need you to talk with some of my friends with the FBI."

"Sure. Sure, I will talk with anyone you ask me to talk with, but this time I want my lawyers present."

"Your lawyers, as in more than one."

"Yes Mr. Logan, we have four lawyers, one for each of us. Ha ha ha ha ha!!!" Williamston went very silent and stone-faced. Tate could no longer get any response from him. The FBI agents rushed into the room and asked Tate to get out. Tate quickly left the room. The agents tried to talk with Williamston, but he would not say a word. He just sat there quietly. Then, four lawyers arrived and entered the room and asked the agents to stop trying to question their clients. It's now revealed that Williamston, Bill Clancy, Sad Clown and Happy Clown, have hired lawyers to represent them, just as if they all were different people.

They all tell the agents, Tate and Captain Carter that their client will no longer be talking with anyone. They will remain silent. With this, they must stop any further questions and Williamston is escorted back to his cell. This was very unusual for one person to have four different lawyers to represent each of his different personalities. The trauma from his childhood experience had fragmented the mind of the murderer into four distinct personalities. It was strange, but not the first time that it's been done. So, for now, the case is on hold and awaiting trial. Now, Tate knows what they are doing. He remembers a large international case that involved a murder. The person charged with the murder confessed and at the trial, it was revealed that the person had many different alter egos. One ego was dominant and dangerous and ruled over the other that was harmless, weak and afraid. They even had two different names for each personality. Tate knows what's coming and he is getting worried. Without being able to question Williamston, the FBI agents leave town. They are planning to have him charged with all the murders that he has confessed to along the east coast. They will use the confession as the evidence, so Tate will be called as the primary witness in all the cases. This could take years to resolve. It will be a nightmare for the local police and the DA's that will prosecute each case, but they are planning to go with it, come what may.

A new DA has taken over the cases, the kidnapping of the old DA and the murder of Tony. Tate will be the primary witness in these cases. But the new DA is reluctant in proceeding with any action that involves the Dooly and Wilson murders until the Fed's get the ball rolling on all the other cases. He keeps saying, those cases have already been resolved and if we come back on them too quickly, we could not only lose those cases, but we could also lose the Williamston case too. Until the Williamston case is resolved, it would not be a good idea. Tate is really having a problem with the way this is going. Court will be coming up next Monday and now everyone is having concerns about how it will go. So, for a week Tate's wondering and worrying about what this guy is up to, but there's nothing anyone can do.

9:00 AM, Monday, September 13, 2007:

The day everyone is waiting for has finally arrived. Everyone is in the courtroom and eager to begin the process. Tate, Captain

Carter and all the other witnesses are ready to testify.   In this case, the defense has waived the right to a hearing.   This seemed a little odd to the DA, but with the confession and all the evidence, it could have been a good move in their favor.   Williamston and all four of his lawyers are also here and ready.
The judge speaks:
   "Will the defendant please rise?"
Williamston, along with his four lawyers, slowly stands up and faces the judge.
The judge speaks:
   "Mr. Williamston, you have been charged with first-degree murder of Tony Johnson. (The murder case will be heard first.) How do you plead?"
   "Not guilty, Your Honor! Not guilty, for me, Sad Clown, Bill Clancy, and Happy Clown!"
The judge has a strange look on his face. He bangs his gavel and says:
   "Counsel for the defense and the DA, please approach the bench."
The four lawyers and the DA approach, and the judge asked;

"What do you think you are doing here? Gentlemen, this had better be good."
Then, the Happy Clown's lawyer said,

"Your Honor, the night of the arrest, Sad Clown was the one that was arrested, and he was advised of his rights. But Your Honor, my client, Happy Clown was not advised of his rights. He was the one that gave a statement of what he thought Sad Clown had done. So, Your Honor, I am requesting that this case be thrown out due to malicious malpractice of justice."
The DA then said;

"Your Honor, this is preposterous, outlandish and totally unacceptable."
The judge quickly denies the request, and everyone is told to return to their seats. A jury must now be selected. This can sometime take a few days, but in this case, it only took about three hours. Now that the jury has been selected, the judge tells the DA to call his first witness.
The DA called Detective Tate Logan to the stand. On the way to the stand, Tate stopped and took the Oath, with his left hand on the

Bible and his right hand raised. He was asked by the Clerk.

"Do you solemnly swear to tell the truth, the whole truth and nothing but the truth, so help you God?"
Tate said,

"Yes." He took a seat on the witness stand.
The DA stood up and walked over to Tate and said:

"Tell the court who you are and what you do for a living."

"I am Detective Tate Logan with the Wilmington Police Department," Tate said with confidence.

"How long have you worked with the Police Department, Mr. Logan?"

"I have been with the Department for about thirty years, and I have worked as a homicide detective for over twenty-five years."

"Detective Logan, tell the court in your own words what you know about this case." Tate tells with detail what he knew about the murder of Tony Johnson. The whole time Tate was testifying, not one objection and not one word from the defense. This was a little different for the DA and Tate. They always have some sort of objection or a display of outrage from the witness. But not this time. After Tate had concluded his testimony, the DA looked at the judge and said.

"No further questions, Your Honor." The judge looked at the defense. At this time, the Happy Clown's lawyer stood up and slowly walked over to Tate. As he walked toward Tate, he stated:

"Detective Logan, you have told us a very convincing story. I must admit, it sounds pretty good, but I have a couple of questions for you. One, when you arrested Mr. Williamston, or Mr. Bill Clancy or Mr. Sad Clown or Mr. Happy Clown, which one did you arrest?"

"Sir, they all may be calling themselves different names, but we all know that I arrested Mr. Williamston, AKA Bill Clancy, AKA Happy Clown, AKA Sad Clown. They all are the same."

"No!! Detective Logan they are very different! To you and maybe the DA, they are the same, but no, Detective Logan, they are very different!!! Detective Logan, when you put the cuffs on the person that you arrested that night inside the RV, what did that person look like?"

"Sir, he was dressed up to look like a clown. He had a clown suit and clown face paint on. But that person is Mr. Williamston."

"Detective, can you point him out here today?"

"Yes." Tate said as he points toward Mr. Williamston.

"That's him sitting over there."

"No, Detective Logan, let me remind you of your testimony. You said, and you are under Oath, and I quote:

'He was dressed in a clown suit and he had a Sad Clown face painted on.'
Now Detective Logan, is that what you said?"

"Yes, I said that, and he did have it on."

"Detective Logan, you also said that you advised the person in the Sad Clown suit of his rights. Is that correct?"

"Yes. I advised him of his rights."

"Detective Logan, I believe that you did advise him of his rights. But let me ask you another question. When you got the confession from the person at the police station that night, who gave it to you?"

"Mr. Williamston did."

"No, Detective! NO! You told us all that, the person called himself the Happy Clown! Now, is that what you told us all?! And Detective Logan, you never read the Happy Clown his Miranda Rights... did you?!!"

"No, but there's no difference, they all are one of the same."

"No further questions, Your Honor. We request that this case be thrown out due to an egregious disregard for my Client's constitutional rights." The lawyer starts quoting case law that involved: 'Dissociative Identity Disorders,' DID and 'Multiple Personality Disorder' MPD.

"Billy Milligan 1978, Billy Joe Harris 2005. And Your Honor, there are many more and Your Honor, my client not only falls under these cases, but more importantly, he

was not even advised of his rights."
The DA is sternly objecting to this. The
judge appears to be a little hesitant on
making a call. He calls the DA and the
Happy Clown's attorney to the bench.
This judge is very young and just getting
started in his career. Maybe, not as wise as
some older judges. So, he tells the two
lawyers:
   "Counsel… to make a claim you are going
to need more than a few old cases. You must
have much more to meet the precedence and
so far, I don't see it. As for Officer Logan
not advising Happy Clown his rights. I am
going to overrule that. And the reason is, no
one has proven that DID or MPD exist in this
case."
Happy Clown's lawyer requested a
continuance, so he can have his client
examined by a professional. The judge
granted his request and set the court date for
two weeks. Tate could not believe what was
going on. The DA and Captain Carter were
also baffled and confused over what was
taking place. As they were leaving the

courtroom, Williamston was being taken back to his cell. As they were going out the door, Williamston looked at Tate and let out that crazy laugh.

"Ha, ha, ha, ha, ha, ha!!!"
Tate slammed his fist on the desk and said:

"That no good rascal is going to get off, I just know it." The DA and Brad were both trying to reassure Tate.

"Tate, this is not over and he's not going to win!" Brad said with confidence.
The DA then said:

"Tate, they are just pulling at straws, they're not going to win this and it's just a cheap lawyer trick."

Chapter twenty-one

8:07 AM, Monday, September 26, 2007:

Tate is to be back in court for the trial of Williamston and he's getting a call from FBI Special Agent Wilkins.

"Tate, I hate to call you on this one but you're not going to believe what I'm about to say. We have not been able to get anyone in any of the murder cases to file charges. They all are telling us that it's political suicide to relitigate these cases. They are not interested in letting anyone in any of these cases go. They all say that they are satisfied that justice was served, and the right people are in jail."

"But all of these people are innocent, and you know it!"

"Yes, we both know it, but try telling that to all these people, the police officers, the DAs and the judges that will look bad if they have to let all these people go. Not to mention the dollar amount on this thing. It would be in the millions and it would take years. Tate, it's not going to happen. You guys have two innocent people in jail yourselves."

This was a big letdown for Tate and a big win for the Thin Man. But Tate's not giving up on his cases. Then, Brad came into his office and asked if he was ready for court. Tate grabbed his case file and evidence and they both go over to the courtroom. On the way, Tate brings Brad up to speed on what the FBI just told him, and Brad, too, was disappointed, but not really surprised.

9:03 AM:

They enter the courtroom and court is already in session. They can see Williamston sitting in the bullpen with his orange jumpsuit on. His four lawyers are sitting at the table for the defense and the DA is sitting at the table to their right. The judge is going over some papers and it's very quiet in the room. Tate and the Captain take a seat behind the DA and as Tate looks toward Williamston, he begins to boil in anger. He knows that this nut has made everyone up and down the east coast look like fools and has gotten away with all those murders. But Tate is hoping and praying that he will not slip out of paying for the murder of his friend and the kidnapping of the DA.

The Judge looks up at the DA and said,
   "Mr. DA, call your case."
The DA then called the case, and Williamston came around and was seated with his lawyers.   The trial was started once more. Now, the lawyer for the Happy Clown called his first witness.

   "Your Honor, I call Dr. Jerry Whitfield." The judge tells Dr. Whitfield to take the oath and the witness stand. Then after taking the oath. Dr. Whitfield takes a seat on the stand. The lawyer asked the Dr. to tell the court about himself and what his findings are in the matter of Mr. Williamston. After giving a long resume on his education and professional experience, the doctor tells all about his research regarding Williamston.

   "…Your Honor, after a very careful and thorough review of Mr. Williamston, I find that he does, in fact, have Multiple Personality Disorder. MPD occurs as a result due to severe trauma. This is considered a mental health disorder. The brain fragments and the original consciousness retreats and the alters are created as a defense mechanism by the brain. Each one of these fragments takes on its own individualized identity. Therefore, Your Honor, Mr. Williamston does in fact have four different and distinct and unique personalities. It all came about when he was a young child. His father was never a role model in his life and almost killed him when he was only nine years old. His mother was a self-centered woman that hated him so much that she made him a part of her sick and perverted games with her lover. She would make her own son watch her have intercourse with her lover whenever her husband was out of town, which was quite often. She dressed him in two different clown suits, with this secret being kept between Reginald, his mother, and her lover.

"So, in an attempt, to remove himself from this behavior and abuse, his brain created these different personalities. It's hard to imagine just how much shame and suffering went on in the mind of that nine-year-old boy. The only escape was to create alters to protect the little boy who was harmed. So, it's my professional opinion that Mr. Williamston had no idea that the Sad Clown was doing the terrible things. Now, the Happy Clown did know, and he did not like what was going on, but he was too afraid to tell anyone. That is until he met Detective Logan. Bill Clancy also knew, but he was just as bad as the Sad Clown. The Happy Clown has an IQ of 76, Bill Clancy has the IQ of 84, while both the Sad Clown and Mr. Williamston share an IQ of 200. But the bad thing here is Bill Clancy and Sad Clown would never let Mr. Williamston come out. They kept him locked away as a way of protecting him, as strange as that may sound."

The Attorney for Williamston asked;

"Dr. Whitfield…does Mr. Williamston have NPD?"

"No…But it is my belief that Mr. Sad

Clown does, in fact, have NPD or Narcissistic Personality Disorder."

The DA stood up and shouted;

"Objection, Your Honor! This is outrageous!"

"Overruled...sit down Mr. DA."

The Defense Attorney asked;

"Dr. Whitfield do you believe that Mr. Williamston has a condition known as, Psychological Trauma?"

"In this case...it is of my professional opinion that he does, in fact, have this disorder."

"Objection. Your Honor! Irrelevant!" The DA said.

"Overruled...continue on." As the judge motioned his hand to the defense attorney. The DA is all worked up and very frustrated. And Tate is beginning to worry that Williamston may get off. Dr. Whitfield was on the stand all morning and gave a great amount of detail to support his findings. Later at about noon, the judge called for a lunch recess. Tate, the DA and Brad went to lunch at the Court-Side Cafe' next to the courthouse.   While sitting there waiting for their food, the DA looked at Tate and asked:

"So, Tate how are the Feds coming with this case?"

"Well Sir, I was hoping that you had forgotten about them."

"Why would I need to forget about them?"

"I talked with them just before we came into court this morning."

"And…?"

"They have scrapped the whole thing."

"What the heck are you saying?!"

"They can't seem to get anyone interested in reopening any of the cases. They are being told that it would be too costly, and it will make everyone involved look bad in the public eye. The cases have all been tried and the people have been convicted. End of conversation. And, that's how it's going to be. Or so they tell me."

The DA is very upset.

"Tate! We may lose this one today and if the jury sends this guy off to the nut house, we are going to not only LOOK, like a bunch of fools, we are going to BE, a bunch of fools!"

Now, Brad has not said a word. He has been deep in thought. But now he speaks:

"Look, Mr. DA… You can beat Williamston, you just got to stay on 'em. Stay on 'em like white on rice. Don't let up!"

Now, this new DA is very accomplished in his field and he's been around for a long time. His name is Wallace Blalock. He's about sixty years old, overweight and has a bald head. He's slow, deliberate and to the point. He has a gruff voice and when he speaks people tend to listen. He is nothing like the DA that let himself get caught by Williamston. He will not give up so easily. He knows he's got a real battle on his hands. After all, this is not a hearing, it's the real thing. He along with Carter and Tate were expecting that the defense would pull these 'DID and MPD' cards at some point. But with the news that the Feds are not pursuing charges for everything else Williamston has done, the wind has been taken from everyone's sails. That news was a big blow to everyone's morale. The injustice of this was astounding and unbelievable.

Back in the courtroom, the judge calls the court to order, and Dr. Whitfield is called back to the stand. He makes a very convincing argument that Williamston does, in fact, have DID, or Dissociative Identity Disorder.

"Yes, Your Honor, Dissociative Identity Dissociation is a type of amnesia that involves the inability to recall important personal information, that would not typically be lost with ordinary forgetting, caused by trauma or stress. The information lost would normally be part of conscious awareness and would be described as autobiographic memory. And your Honor, with the type of abuse Mr. Williamston suffered as a child he would definitely have reason to have this disorder."

When he finished testifying, the DA asked a few questions, but he knew this guy had done a good job. He surmised that he would only make things worse by questioning him further.

He has also requesting the opportunity to use

a well-known psychiatrist to counter Dr. Whitfield. This will delay the trial for another week.

For the next week, Tate has a hard time sleeping. All he can think about is how Williamston has been able to pull this off, and how he is laughing and thumbing his nose at everyone. It's a crazy game and this nut seems to be winning. But Tate's not one to give up so easily.

Court will be starting back up first thing tomorrow morning and Tate's ready and so is the new DA. Dr. William Myers another famous psychiatrist will be taking the stand for the state.

Tate and Brad are at the Red Wing Restaurant, having a nice meal. Tate ordered his wings and burger combo, and Brad ordered a chicken salad.

"Tate, how do you think this case is going to go?"

"Brad, I am so worried. He might get off, and I'm just beside myself."

"You have to let it go. If he gets off, he gets off. You've done your job."

"I know…I know, but it still gets to me that he's already gotten by with everything else!"

"Tate! You've got to just go in there and do what you do. No one is as good in court as you, and you know that." Regardless, if Williamston gets off or he's convicted, Tate will have to testify one more time.

"Thanks, but this is different. The guy has played this game and he is so smart. There's nothing wrong with him. He's just a homicidal maniac. A cold-blooded killer and the thought of him going to a mental hospital just makes me so damn angry! And I know, I've got to let up."

"Tate just go in and do your thing and stop obsessing over it. You have the DNA from the crap you found, you have the confession, you have witnesses, you have video of 'em all over the place. The only thing they have is this Dr. Whitfield, and Myers should knock him out."

"But I am worried about this young judge. He's acting like he does not know what's going on half the time."

"He's smarter than he looks, and we just

have to trust that he's going to do the right thing."

"You know Brad, I have been looking and I have also worked with the FBI on trying to find someone that Williamston is close too, but we can't come up with anyone. If we could find anyone that he knows, we might be able to get them to testify against him. But we just can't find anyone. He has not talked to anyone from jail but his lawyers. He hasn't made a single phone call from jail, not even to his lawyers."

"What about Richmond, where he grew up? Does he own the property that his father owned or what?"

"One of the agents at the FBI went to the house. He said that it looked to be abandoned and was in very bad shape. It was so bad that he was afraid to even go into it."

"Well, did he go in or not?"

"From what he told me…he never went into the house."

"Tate, if we leave now, we can get there in four hours. I can call one of the Richmond Police Detectives to meet us there and we can go in and see if we can find anything that may help us in this case."

"Brad, I am ready to go, but I really think it's a wash. I just think we would be wasting our time. But heck, let's go. I need to get away from here for a while anyway."

Chapter twenty-two

After a long drive, they arrive at the address of the big old house that Williamston lived in as a child. About twenty minutes before they arrived, Tate called the Richmond Police Department and asked the Detective to meet them at the house. So, when they arrived, Detective Buddy Jackson of the Richmond Police Department was waiting for them in the driveway. This place is in very bad shape. It has tall weeds in the yard, vines growing all around the house, and cobwebs in every corner. Herman Munster's home would be a step up from this place. After talking with Jackson, they went into the house through the front door. Due to the house being declared abandoned, a search warrant is not needed. Now, the three men are standing in what was the living room. They see old furniture, old pictures, cobwebs, dust and dirt all around. "Be careful fellows, this floor may just fall through at any time."

Jackson said.

"Let's find the bedroom where the murders took place over thirty years ago." Tate said.

"It's upstairs fellows, follow me. I was not on the force back then, but I once lived down the road from one of the detectives that worked the case. He told me all about what happened. Detective Scott Reed was the investigating officer. He's retired now, but he lives about two miles from here. After we check this out, we can go by and talk with him, if you like."

"Sure thing." Brad said as they went slowly up the stairs.
When they got to the top of the stairs they turned to the left and headed down to the bedroom. When they pushed the creaky door open, they were surprised to see the clean and neat room. It looked as though someone had been keeping it in the original condition it had been before the murders had taken place. As they go in, Tate spots a big trunk at the foot of the big bed.

"Wonder what's in the trunk guys," Brad said.

"I don't know, but I'm going to find out," Tate said as he bent down to open it.

As Tate opened the trunk, they could not believe their eyes. There was a gallon jar filled with what looked to be alcohol. Also, inside the jar were several human fingers. There must have been from eighty to a hundred fingers in that jar. While on the left side of the trunk, were two, small clown suits along with the clown mask, one sad face and one happy face. It looks like our Williamston has been coming here very often. This was quite a surprise to these detectives.

"I'm calling for CSI and backup. We just fell into something big here fellows." Jackson said. Just after the call was made, they heard a door slam downstairs. Tate and the other two men looked at each other wide-eyed and then they all ran down the stairs. As they get to the bottom of the stairs, Tate can see an image running around the house toward the old log building at the rear of the big house. The three ran out into the yard to the log house. They can see someone go in the front door. They all ran to the door and Detective Jackson, out of breath, yells:

"Come out! And come out with your hands where we can see them."

"I'm coming out, please don't shoot me!" A weak male voice replied from inside the old cabin. Then the old weathered wooden door slowly open's, and an old black man comes out, with his hands up.

"My goodness! It's the old black man that Thin Man was impersonating." Tate said with dismay.

"And look, his right index finger is gone!"

"We thought you had been killed by Williamston the second." Brad said.

"No Sir. No Sir, that was my brother."

"What happened to your finger?" Tate asked.

"That's a long story, a long, long story."

"We got time. Why don't you tell us about it? You can start by telling us what your name is."

"My name is Alfred Suggs. Can I put my hands down now?"

"Sure. Go ahead. By the way, when was

the last time you saw Mr. Williamston, III?"

"He comes around every once and a while. He brings me food and he kind'a looks after me with things. Things that I need from time to time. He's very good to me, cause, I don't have nobody else to help me. But it's been a while. I ain't seen him in over a month."

"You look like you could use something cold to drink and maybe something hot to eat." Jackson said.

"Yes Sir, I sure could."

Brad, Tate, and Mr. Suggs load up in the car and drove to a little country diner just down the road. Detective Jackson stayed at the house to wait for CSI. As Tate is leaving, they can see that CSI have arrived. They will be going over the area with a fine-tooth comb. It's a short drive to the diner and no one was saying much while on the way. So, Tate called Jim with the FBI and gave him an update on what was going on. The FBI will also respond to the old house to take assessment of the scene and then take custody of any evidence found. The locals may not like it, but the Feds override any local law on this one.

At the diner, they sit in a booth near the rear of the restaurant so they could have privacy. Brad then tells Tate and Mr. Suggs, to get whatever they want. Mr. Suggs ordered six hot dogs, all the way and a thirty-two-ounce beer. Tate and Brad get some coffee. Before the food comes out, they start working on Mr. Suggs…You know the good cop, bad cop thing.

Tate's the good cop.

"We just want to help you." Tate said softly.

"But if you don't work with us, we'll put your sorry behind in jail!" Brad said with an authoritative voice.

They could see Mr. Suggs was getting nervous, and they know that he will have a lot to say. The only problem was, would he talk? The food came out and Mr. Suggs starts eating. As he was eating, Mr. Suggs started talking. He was just rambling around and not telling anything about Williamston. So, Brad turned up the pressure;

"Look man! Why are you acting like we

are a couple of fools?! Those fingers in that jar alone could put your ass on death row!" Mr. Suggs just sat there, and now; he's not saying anything. So, Tate softly said;

"Mr. Suggs you need to help us out here. If you don't start telling us what you know, my Captain here is going to arrest you and I won't be able to help you. Please, for your own sake…please just tell us what you know about what Williamston's been doing." Mr. Suggs looks at Tate and said:

"Can you keep him from arresting me if I tell you what I know?" Tate reached over and touched Suggs on the shoulder and softly said;

"If you tell us the truth…I give you my word that no one will be arresting you. Right, Captain?" Brad takes a long look at Suggs and said;

"Sure, but if you tell us one lie, just one, there is no deal!" Mr. Suggs thought for a minute and said:

"Okay I will tell you the truth, but if he finds out, I am a dead man." Tate looked at Suggs and said; "Look, Mr. Suggs, your food is getting cold, go on and start eating while you tell us what we need to know." Mr. Suggs took a bite of hotdog, a big sip of beer and then started talking. Man alive, he was eating like a horse, and he was also telling the news. It seems that it was his twin brother that Williamston's father killed, the day he walked in the bedroom. And the missing finger from Mr. Suggs, that was just a coincidence. He lost it in a lawnmower accident. (So much for the long, long story.) When Williamston III, turned twenty years old, he sought Mr. Suggs out and started looking after him. Williamston had lived with his grandfather until then. No one had been in the house from the time of the murders.

"Yeah, when he found me, I was in jail. He got me out and started looking after me. He paid the lawyer and got me out of a B&E (Break and Entering) charge. He took me out to the old house and set up the old building out back as my living quarters. It ain't much, but it was better than what I had. And all I had to do was keep that bedroom clean. I'm also supposed to keep people away from the house. But I messed up today, didn't I?"

"We have a burning question for you," Brad said.

"Yes Sir."

"Tell us about all those fingers in that big jar, in the trunk in the bedroom."
Now, there's a change with the old fellow. He starts to get a little nervous and he stopped talking. He knows something that he obviously doesn't want to tell. Tate tells him that if he does not tell what he knows about those fingers, and his boss, then he will be in a lot of trouble.

"I can't tell you! He's crazy! He will kill me for sure and he'll kill y'all too. You don't know just how hateful and mean that man can be. He's smart too. He caught me in a lie, and he locked me in my own little house for two weeks. And he told me that if I ever told him a lie or did anything that he did not like, he would kill me and chop me up and feed me to the gators down in Florida."

"Look, Mr. Suggs, he can't hurt you or anyone else. He's in jail and he will be going to prison for a long time. He may even get death row. But you need to tell us something that we don't already know. Now, if you don't tell us the truth and if you don't tell us everything, you may be joining your boss in jail and possibly death row. Do you understand?" Tate said in a very stern manner.

"Yes Sir."

"Just start from the beginning."

"One thing I can say…he brags to me all the time about the things he does."

"What kind of things are you talking about?"

"I just can't do it…I just can't tell."

"Look, Mr. Suggs, you have to do this, it's all over now."

"No! No! No! You don't know this man, if I tell you anything about him, he's going to kill me, and I know he'll do it!"

"Okay, have it your way, but we will be taking you in for accessory and you can join Williamston in jail." Tate says as he pulls out his handcuffs.

"What you going to do?"

"We're going to have to arrest you."

"But I did not do anything, I didn't kill nobody!!!"

"Mr. Suggs, I'll give you one more chance and only one…now, what's it going to be?"

"Okay, I'll tell you everything that I know, but please don't put them cuffs on me."
As Tate put the cuffs back in his pocket, he tells Mr. Suggs:

"Okay, we're going down to the Police Station and we are going to take a statement from you. You better tell us everything."

Chapter twenty-three

Tate, Brad, and Mr. Suggs are sitting in the interrogation room. Suggs has agreed to go back with them to North Carolina and the trip has been arranged. But before they go Suggs wants to tell everything he knows about Williamston. Tate and Brad are ready to listen.

"You might think he's crazy, but you would be wrong, very wrong. He's not crazy and he will make all of you look like fools." Suggs said as he lights up a cigarette.

"Oh, we know he's not crazy and he's already made us look bad," Tate replied.

"Every time he's ever killed someone, he has bragged to me about how he did it and how he framed some poor soul for it. He also bragged about making the police look like fools. All of them fingers...he showed me every single one. You know...he's not but one person. He's not two different clowns and as for that name, 'Bill Clancy,' that was an old man that used to work for his father years ago. Now, why he uses it, I don't know. Bill died when Williamston was seven years old. He was a good man, from what I remember."

"You know you will have to testify to what you are telling us." Brad said.

"If you do, you will be fine, but with what you are telling us, if you don't testify, then you will be in a lot of trouble." Tate explained.

"Yes, Sir, I know…he's going to kill me anyway. I know he will, and he may kill you, too."

Tate asked Mr. Suggs:

"Has he bragged about using the clown suits and his many different disguises?"

"Yes Sir. He's very proud of that. He said that would keep him off death row if he ever got caught. He would tell me all about how he could fool, even the best doctors and lawyers. And he will!"

Brad replied:

"No Mr. Suggs, with your testimony, he's

not going to get away with anything."

"But he's killed almost a hundred people and he's a psychopath."
Suggs talked for a long time and he gave them information and insight into Williamston.

"When did Williamston start killing people?" Tate asked Mr. Suggs.

"Well…you know, for the first ten years he was very good to me, and I don't think he was killing people during that time. But he started acting up. He began to change. He started getting hateful and mean. I don't know what happened to him, but it was very, very bad. He would tell me things that I knew were wrong. He played games with me and I knew I could not win those games. He was just too smart for me. He even told me that I was no fun at all. He really changed in the last ten years."

"Do you know where Williamston lived or where he was staying? Did he ever tell you anything about his life? Did he have any friends or family that you know of?" Tate asked.

"I don't know …he never talked about anyone. He never said anything about where he lived. He would just show up here with one or two fingers, brag and then put them in the jar. Sometimes, he just showed up and had me cook for him. He never stayed overnight. He never came around with anyone else. He was always alone when he came. But like I said, the first ten years was very good and the last ten years…he was awful."

"Why did he have you keep his mother's and father's bedroom so clean, but let everything else go down so bad?"

Brad asked.

"I don't know…I just don't know. He would go into that room and stay for hours and each time he went in alone. He always told me to stay out. I would not go near that room when he told me to stay out."

Tate continued:

"Mr. Suggs, I want you to think and really think about this before you say anything. Can you remember anything that Williamston did that might have been connected to the murders?"

Mr. Suggs pondered and answered:

"I can't think of anything else. No, wait, I do remember something, but it did not have anything to do with any murders."

"What was that, Mr. Suggs?" Brad asked.

"Well...ahh... I don't know, it's not a big deal. Just forget about it..."

"No, No, it may be more than you think, just tell us what it was." Tate said.

Mr. Suggs tells Tate and Brad of a strange encounter with Williamston:

"This happened about ten years ago when I noticed him becoming mean. He came out to see me and when he came in, he had a big suitcase in his hand. I did not know what was in it but when he brought it in, he set it over next to the door. I thought about it, but I was not about to ask him anything about it. He opened a bottle of wine and asked me to go into the kitchen and get us two glasses. So, I did and when I brought them back, he sent me back into the kitchen to get some paper towels. So, I did as he asked. When I got back, he already had the wine in the

glasses. As I walked into the room, he gave me a glass so we could make a toast. The toast was funny."
Williamston said;

"'Here's to you… and here's to me… and if we ever disagree… here's to me… and the heck with you.'"
Suggs continued:

"We drank the wine. The next thing I remember, I was waking up on the couch in my little living room and Williamston was gone."

"What do you think happened during the time you were out?" Brad said as he looked over at Tate'

"I am not sure, but it happened again about one year ago. He did the same thing, the case, wine and all. During the time I was out, I had a dream. I was dreaming that I was being suffocated in a big mud hole. I was sinking, and my face was the last thing that went under the mud. The funny thing about that dream…my face felt very clean as if I had washed it several times. Yes, it was very strange. To this day, I just don't know how and why I let just one glass of wine do me that way."

Now, Tate and Brad knew what had happened to him, but they remained silent. They look at each other with a knowing look that they must get Suggs back to Wilmington to testify. They don't have a lot of time. So, with a court order from a judge, they head back to Wilmington with Suggs.

After driving through the night, they arrived at the jail the next morning at about 2:00 AM. They locked Mr. Suggs up and headed home for a little sleep before court at 9:00 AM. At 8:30 AM, they meet with the new District Attorney with the news of their witness.

"Are you sure this guy will testify?"

"Yeah, he has promised us that he'll tell everything he knows in court." Brad said.

"Okay, if we can get him on the stand with this and he does not break, it will be really good for our case. But he's a hostile witness, and you know how that can end up. He could make us look just as bad as Williamston has made us look. It's a gamble and I am willing to go with it."

"He does have all the facts and he's seen all those fingers. He's been told in detail of each case." Tate said.

"But Tate, this guy has not told you anything about our cases. After all, he did tell you that he's not seen Williamston in over a month…so, he has nothing, nothing at all."

"Wait, wait just a minute, if you can get what he's done in the other cases along with all those fingers in that jar…then, you could show that he had malice and intent to commit the crimes in our cases." Captain Carter said.

"We can try but, you know they are going to object. You have done a good job getting this Suggs witness here but it all may be for naught."

"If all these murder cases could be reopened and the Feds were willing to work with us, we could get him. I mean, we could get him good." Tate said with a sigh.

"Fellows, I'm going to approach the judge with this and just maybe we can get Suggs on the stand. I'll also try to get a continuance,

so we can prepare a disclosure statement for
the defense."

Chapter twenty-four

9:30 AM

Court has been called back in session. Mr. Suggs is nervously sitting with Tate in the courtroom. As Williamston is brought into the courtroom, he quickly spots Suggs. The look on his face was one for the books, but the look he gave Suggs was one for the ages. If looks could kill, Suggs would have fallen over dead. He almost got up and ran out. Tate was holding on to him and he was holding hard.

"I can't do it! I just can't! He's going to kill me for sure...I just know he'll do it!" Suggs said with a great tone of fear on his face.

"He's not going to kill anyone else. We've got him! The only way he'll kill you, is if you go to jail with him. If you testify you will not go, but he will, but if you don't testify, you will end up with him in jail, so it's up to you."

"Okay, it looks like I'm going to have to testify, but I sure don't want too. You just don't know how smart he is. He can get out of this and there will not be a thing anyone can do."

"Trust me Mr. Suggs, we are going to get Williamston this time. You can count on it." Then, after a few minutes, the judge calls for the case to begin and a jury needed to be selected. This took all day and part of the next. The trial began. Every time there was a recess and Williamston had to be taken out of the courtroom, he would look at Tate and Suggs and let out that laugh. This was getting on most everyone's nerves, especially Tate and Suggs. Tate's doing all he can to calm Mr. Suggs, but poor old Suggs is really having a hard time. Tate has been taking Mr. Suggs to breakfast, lunch and supper every day and Suggs is eating like a horse each time. Tate's also letting Mr. Suggs room with him at his place. But things are not going as well as Tate hoped it would.

The DA is now ready to put Dr. Myers on the stand to make his argument. After being sworn in, he testifies to his findings. The defense objects to almost everything he says. The judge overruled some and sustained some. Something was just not right with this judge, he seemed confused at times.

After Dr. Myers had finished, the lawyer for Williamston was asked if he wanted to cross examine the witness. But for some reason, he declined. The DA called Mr. Alfred Suggs to the stand. The defense objected.

"Your Honor! We object, this man is a friend of our client's and he has no education. He's not competent to testify."

"Overruled, he may take the stand."

Mr. Suggs was sworn in and he took the stand. He told the story of Williamston's activities and how he controlled him. He described how he bragged about killing people, and fooling law enforcement. The defense objected to almost every word, but the judge allowed all of what he had to say. He was a very convincing witness and you could see that the jury seemed to be impressed. Then once more the defense declined to cross examine the witness. Now this is very strange. The DA, Brad and Tate are all wondering just what the defense is up to.

The two sides are ready to give their final closing arguments to the jury before they would deliberate. The defense goes first and only Williamston's attorney gets up to speak to the jury. And the jury has been given a choice when making their conclusion. The choices were, guilty of murder in the first degree, not guilty of murder in the first degree, or not guilty due to reason of insanity.

The attorney walks up and down in front of the jury for a while before he said a word. Then, he looks at each one and said;

"Ladies and Gentlemen, you have heard all the so-called evidence, that the DA has presented. You also have heard from Dr. Whitfield, a man of the utmost, professional qualifications. It's as clear as a bell that Mr. Williamston had no idea what the Sad clown was doing. So, it's quite simple, you must vote not guilty. Incidentally, when Detective Logan was questioning Mr. Williamston, he was violating his constitutional rights!

"He never even advised him of his rights! This alone should have thrown the case out of court! Now, you also need to remember the poor old Mr. Suggs. It's clear that he was told what to say. Mr. Williamston has looked after this poor man like a brother. It's clear that he was forced to testify! The poor man was scared to death! So, it's really very simple. You must vote, not guilty!

"Now, I will agree that my client has some very severe mental problems. But please I beg you…he does not belong in prison! Sure, he needs help, but ladies and gentlemen, he will not get the help that he so desperately needs in prison. Just think about that little, nine-year-old boy and the pain he must have had to endure. Sure, I could go on and on. I just want you to do the right thing here…that's all. Have some mercy on this poor man. Imagine you are this nine-year-old boy. You are that little child that has suffered this enormous pain and suffering that was placed on you by all the adults you trust. You have been scarred for life. Please, I beg of you, do the right thing and vote not guilty." Then, he takes one last, longing and lingering look at each person on the jury. He walks back to his seat and sits down. The judge asked;

"Council are you finished?"

"Yes, Your Honor, the defense rests." This summation seemed very short to Tate. A normal summation would usually take a lot longer. Yes, this was very strange. Tate looks at Brad, leans over and whispers;

"Too short…somethings not right…" Brad just looks at Tate with a surprised look and shrugged his shoulders.

The Judge tells the District Attorney to proceed.

"Yes, Your Honor, thank you." The DA stood up and walked over to the jurors.

"Ladies and Gentlemen, good afternoon. I know you all must be ready to get this over with, and I want to thank you for your time.

"But Ladies and Gentlemen you have a

duty here today. Yes, you must vote guilty in this case. It is abundantly clear that the accused is guilty beyond the shadow of any reasonable doubt. His confession alone makes it very clear, that he committed the crime.

"Sure, the other side brought in a smart doctor to say what they want him to say. We also had a very smart doctor that told a much different story. So, who should you believe, their doctor or our doctor? You also heard from Mr. Suggs, which really was a very good witness for our side. He has known the defendant for decades. And Mr. Suggs has a real fear that if Williamston is turned loose that he may try to kill him for just telling the truth. Also, please remember the testimony. of Detective Logan. He showed us a clear picture of what Mr. Williamston had done.

"Make no bones about it…Williamston's guilty and the citizens need to be protected from him. So, with that said…Ladies and Gentlemen, you must find Mr. Williamston guilty of murder in the First Degree."
The DA looks at each person once more and

he looks right into their eyes. He emphasizes;

"Guilty! Guilty! Do the right thing!"
But unlike the lawyer for the defense, the DA is not finished. He goes into extreme detail of what Williamston did. He presented graphic photos of the crime scene. He showed each piece of evidence and explained in detail what it meant to prove that Williamston is a murderer. His summation lasted for two hours.

"Ladies and Gentlemen, once more I ask of you to honor the truth. Guilty! Guilty! Guilty! The evidence shows only one conclusion, Guilty!" Now he walks by the jury and with one last plea, as he slowly looks at each person.

"Guilty…Guilty…Guilty."
He then walked back over to his seat, looked at the judge and said; "The Prosecution rests Your Honor."
The judge briefly gave the jury instructions and told the bailiff to escort them to the jury room for deliberations. He called for a recess until the jury comes back with their verdict.

As everyone started to leave the courtroom, Tate gets a bad feeling, in his gut. He knows that something's not right. But he just can't put his finger on it. The DA looks at Tate and says;

"Tate, you did good on this case, I feel good that we are going to get a conviction here, today."

"I sure wish I felt the same way, but something's not right." Tate said.

"What do you mean, Something's not right?"

"I don't know, and I hope that it's just one of those things, that's all. I mean, I just don't know."

"Let's go across the street and get something to drink." Brad said as he stood up.

For the next hour, they sat drinking sweet tea and talking about what Tate was going to do with Suggs. They get the call, that the jury has come back with a verdict. It is time to return to the courtroom. They are hoping for guilty, of murder in the first degree. But they just don't know. And Tate… well, he still has that nagging feeling in his gut that something is just not right.

As they sit in the courtroom, the jury files in. Some of them have a bewildered look on their faces and some look frustrated. This does not look good to Tate. The judge asked the question:

"Ladies and Gentlemen of the Jury. Have you reached a verdict?" The Forman of the Jury stands up and with a smile on his face and said:

"Yes, Your Honor, we have. We find the defendant not guilty."

The courtroom erupted. Everyone was in shock, how the heck could this be? What in the heck just happened? Tate and the DA were in disbelief. Williamston looked at Tate and starts that crazy laugh. "Hahahahah!" Mr. Suggs fell into the floor as if he were having a heart attack.

"I told you that he would get off and now he's going to kill me!" Suggs said in a loud cry. Brad looked at Tate, and said:

"What in the world is going on here?"

"I don't know Brad, but I can't believe

what just happened."

The judge is banging his gavel and yelling: "Order! Order, in the Courtroom!"

Slowly, the people in the room settled down. The judge gave a date for the trial of Williamston in the case of kidnapping the DA. It will start tomorrow morning at 9:30. A different jury will have to be selected and everything will start over once more. Tate and Brad know that someone has gotten to one or more of the jury members for this not guilty to come and to come so quickly. The case was just too solid. But they have no clue who has done it. Maybe, Williamston has paid someone to bribe or threaten someone on the jury. But it will all start again in the morning, and they will be on the lookout. For now, it looks like it's going to be another long night for everyone and Tate's going to have a hard time controlling Mr. Suggs.

Tate and Mr. Suggs stop at the Blue Crab to have supper. Man, that Suggs can eat, especially for someone that has been so afraid. They both have a good meal and head over to Tate's place for the night. All Suggs can say, is.

"He's going to kill me, he's going to kill me, and I know he's going to do it." Tate kept telling him to hang on…just a few more days and Williamston would be going to prison. But Suggs was not having that, no way. It was a long night. Suggs was having nightmares all night, waking Tate by yelling, "No! NO!"

Now, after a long sleepless night and a little breakfast, they are ready to head over to the courthouse. Tate looks like hell and Suggs looks no better. This case went pretty much like the last case. The DA that had been kidnapped took the stand and did a great job with his testimony. He was very convincing and made a great witness. Tate also told the story and was very convincing. This time the jury was kept closed and no one was able to get to any of them. After about three days, the case ended. The jury was sent into the jury room to deliberate. This time it took several hours, with the Forman requesting several items related to the case. With tension heavy in the air, the jury came back into the court room. The judge asked the Forman;

"Do you have a verdict?"
The Forman stood up and said;

"Yes, Your Honor we do." The Judge asked;

"What is your verdict?"
The Forman said; "Your Honor, we the jury find the defendant Reginal Albert Williamston III, not guilty by reason of insanity."

"What?! What has just happened?" Tate is upset, and so are Suggs and Brad. The courtroom is all in an up-roar again and the Judge is banging his gavel and yelling,

"Order! Order in the courtroom!"

"What happened!?" Tate said. Williamston is laughing like crazy and pointing right at Suggs.

"Ha ha ha ha ha. You will pay! You will pay!!" He yells as they take him from the courtroom,

"I told y'all that he was going to get off and I know he'll be out in no time. He's going to kill us all!" Suggs said as he slumped over like he was having another heart attack.

"Mr. Suggs are you okay?"

"Yes, Detective Logan I'm okay."

"Don't worry Mr. Suggs, Tate will be looking after you. Won't you Tate?" Brad said with a smile. Well, now Tate has got to find out what to do with Mr. Suggs. So, in the meantime, he's going to let Suggs stay with him.

For the next week, Tate's guest, Mr. Suggs, stayed around the apartment cleaning and cooking for Tate. He turned out to be a very good cook. Suggs could be a high paid chef if he wanted to be one. But he does not have the desire to be a chef. Brad's even been over a few times and has also enjoyed Suggs' good cooking. Tate knows that something will have to be done about Mr. Suggs. He can't go back to Richmond, and he has no family or friends to look after him. Suggs is scared to death that Williamston is going to get out of the mental hospital and kill him. Tate is also very concerned about this and he's trying his best to find Suggs a safe place to stay. Brad has asked Suggs to stay with him so he would feel a little better. There is a home for people that are under witness protection. It's kind of a safe house. They can only keep him there for a few days before he would have to be moved to a permanent location. That's what Tate wants to do. However, Suggs is not a good match for this program, so Tate and Brad are taking turns keeping him and moving him about. They continue to tell Suggs to be careful. They don't want him to go anywhere without either of them along. And mostly, he does what they ask, but there are times when he will not listen. Once Tate came in from work early and found the front door standing open. Tate hit the roof and told Suggs that he had to be more careful.

Only a few weeks after Williamston had been locked away, Tate gets a call that Williamston has escaped. His whereabouts are unknown. Tate knows that this is bad news, very bad news. He has got to tell Mr. Suggs and he knows that he's not going to take it very well. It's got to be done, so he heads to his place to tell him the bad news. When he arrives, Mr. Suggs was hard at it, cooking and cleaning just like usual. Tate's also going to have to do something with Suggs. He just can't stay with him and Brad any longer.

"Mr. Suggs, you better sit down, I have some bad news."

"No! No! I know what you're going to tell me! He's got out! Right!?"

"Yes, he has escaped, and no one knows where he is. You know that he's not coming here, and you will be safe with me."

"What about you? He hates you just as much as he hates me. Neither one of us will be safe."

"I am working on finding you a safe place, but you are going to have to work with me."

"When and where am I going to go? And who's going to look after me?"

"I am working on it. Until I can get you out, and when I'm away from here, you need to keep the doors locked. Don't answer the door to anyone. Do you understand?"

"Yes Sir, I understand, but he's going to

kill us both and I just know it!"

As hard as Tate tried, he just could not get through to Mr. Suggs. Tate wants to put Mr. Suggs in protective custody at the jail, but Suggs would not have it. The man was a nervous wreck... a real basket case. Tate was at a loss for words. He just did not know what to do. Yes, it was a long night, with Suggs having nightmares and Tate tossing and turning. Morning came quickly, and Tate must get to work, but what was he going to do with Suggs?

"Mr. Suggs, I've got to go to work and you are going to have to stay here. Just don't open that door for anyone, but me. Do you understand?"

"Okay, but he's going to get me...if not today...it will be soon...I just know it." Tate leaves his place and heads to work. On the way to work, he calls Brad on the cell phone.

"Brad, have you heard anything about Williamston?"

"No, have you?"

"No, not a word, and Suggs is all torn up.

He's about to go crazy and I can't seem to get him straight to save my life. I can't make him go into protective custody at the county jail and I can't get him into any other program."

Brad and Tate are dead in the middle of another murder case and they don't have time to worry about Williamston. Tate calls Suggs several times to check on him and so far, he seems to be okay. So, after a very busy day, they call it quits and head home. The first time Tate talked with Mr. Suggs this morning, Suggs was planning a nice meal for dinner tonight and Tate's ready for it. Steak and lobster as the main course, and a fresh salad with Mississippi Mud cake for dessert. Williamston was not on Tate's mind. All he can think about is what he is going to have for supper.

Tate approaches his front door and he turned the key to the lock. He could not help but think about how upset Suggs was when he heard Williamston had escaped from the mental institution. But Tate feels confident that Williamston's more than likely out of the country by now.   He could escape with all his money and different disguises. He would have no problem getting away. As Tate walked into his living room, he can hear Suggs in the kitchen. He's hard at it again, cooking and rattling those pots and pans. He can now see Suggs over by the sink…

"Suggs! I'm home!"   Suggs waves his left hand over his head, with his back towards Tate, but he did not say anything. Now, this did not seem like Suggs. He always turned to speak to Tate as Tate entered the room. Tate thought, *he seems to be very busy today.* Tate turned the TV on and sat down to catch the evening news. Now, Tate can see Suggs moving around in the kitchen, but he can only see him from the chest up. Something's not right with his new friend... he's not singing and talking like usual.

"Suggs, what's wrong with you Man!" But Suggs says nothing, he just waves his left hand as if he wants Tate to come and eat. So, Tate gets up and walks into the dining room to eat. As he sits, Suggs comes in with a large bowl of salad that he sets on the table.

Tate noticed that Suggs has oven mitts on each hand, but that's nothing new. He often has those mitts on to handle the hot stuff. Suggs goes back into the kitchen and quickly returns with a large pot of hot clam chowder. As he sets it on the table the mitt on his right-hand falls off and hits the floor.
In a state of shock…Tate reaches for his gun, as he sees the right index finger on Williamston's hand. It's not Suggs and it's not going to be good. As Tate's reaching for his gun, Williamston throws the hot pot of clam chowder at him. Somehow, Tate dodged the pot, but Williamston is headed towards the bedroom. Tate fires off three shots, but he misses each time. Williamston locks the bedroom door and is now barking out that crazy laugh. "Ha Ha Ha Ha Ha!!"

Chapter twenty-five

Tate is now having a flashback moment of when he was suckered by the Thin Man in the room at the top of the steps. He's determined to not let that happen again.

"Williamston, you're under arrest!"

"Catch me if you can! You, big dumb jerk!"

"Come out, I don't want to kill you!"

"Where is Suggs? Mr. Logan, what did you do with my man Suggs? Ha Ha Ha Ha!!!"

"Okay, Williamston! Come on out! You can't get away and the SWAT team is on the way!" As Tate dialed 911 on his cell phone, he has no idea what this guy is going to do or what he's done to Suggs. The dispatch officer said;

"911, what is your emergency?" Tate tells the officer to get the SWAT team to his place

ASAP. After talking with the 911 officer, Tate yells to Williamston.

"Come out with your hands up and stop that stupid laugh!"

"Ha Ha Ha Ha!!"

"Make it easy on yourself! Come on out, the SWAT team is on the way!"

"Okay, okay I'll come out, please don't shoot me." The doorknob slowly turns, and the door begins to open, and Williamston's hands are presented to Tate. Now Tate must be very careful because he knows just how dangerous he can be.   As Tate grabs Williamston's hand to put the cuff on. Williamston does a slick move and knocks Tate to the floor. Tate's gun hits the floor and slides across the room and hits the wall. Now, Tate is fighting for his life and this crazy man is laughing.

"Ha Ha Ha Ha Ha Ha!!!"

As Williamston is laughing, Tate's in a blur, his vision is fading as he is falling to the floor.

"Mr. Logan! Mr. Logan! Wake up! Wake up!" The SWAT team member is yelling.

Then Tate starts coming to.

"What happened!" Tate said with a very confused look on his face.

"When we got here your front door was standing open and you were out on the floor."

"Mark! Get in here! There's a body in the spare bedroom," another SWAT team member yelled. (It's Mr. Suggs and he has an ice pick stuck into his ear and it's buried up to the shaft.)

No, not again...how can he keep doing this to me, Tate is thinking.

As he gets to his feet, Brad comes running through the front door.

"Tate! Tate, are you okay?"

"Yes...Yes, I am okay. He's done it again."

"Tate, I can't believe you let this guy get to you again!"

"Well, he did, and he's killed Suggs."

"Just how did he manage to get the upper hand?"

"He was disguised as Suggs when I got home. I knew something was not right. I knew Suggs was not acting right. But when I got a look at his right index finger, I knew it was Williamston. He nearly got me with a pot of scolding hot clam chowder. I shot at him three times, but I know I missed each time. And somehow, he got the drop on me when I went to cuff him."

"Oh Tate, I should have told you, Williamston has a third-degree black belt."

"Gee…Thanks a lot for telling me!" Now, there's an APB out for Williamston and everyone's on high alert. This is not good for the police department or the community. Williamston has got to be caught. It's getting very personal for Tate and Brad. Williamston has made them look like fools at every turn and they are at their wits end with this psychopath.
It's back to work and Tate and Brad are working on the new murder case. They are also looking for Williamston as hard as possible, but nothing is happening. This is driving Tate crazy, but there's nothing more he can do. He knows, that Williamston will show up at any time and he will be continuing this crazy game between he and

Tate. He knows that because Williamston did not kill him when he had the chance. Now all Tate can do is obsess over this nightmare and try to second guess what he has been doing wrong. It's hard enough, concentrating on the work at hand, with this hanging over his head, but he's got to get going. He makes a quick call to Brad and they're headed to eat lunch. The Burgers and Dogs is another place they both like to visit. Man, the burgers at this place are as big as the plates they are served on. They are made the old fashion way, mustard, slaw, chili, and onions and you can smell them cooking a mile before you get there.

They both walk in the front door, and the waitress yells their order even before they can tell her. The usual two burgers, all the way with fries and a coke on the side. They seat themselves and a few minutes later the sexy waitress (Brenda) brings their food out. As usual, Tate's acting like he's hitting on her, but everyone knows that he's just joking with her.

"You know that I've always loved you, you

sexy thing you." Tate said as he looks
Brenda up and down.

"Tate, when are you going to marry me?"

"One day, my love, one day and you better
get ready for me, my love."

"Sure, you are, sure you're just leading me
on, and you know it," as she giggles.

"Now, you know I love you."

"Tate cut it out, people are watching you
and you know we have an image to keep up."
Brad said, with a chuckle.

"Okay…Okay Brad, you're right, I need to
cut it out."

Now as they slowly eat their food, Tate asked
Brad a question that has been bothering him
for days.

"Brad, what's Williamston got against me?
Why is he after me? And why is he making
me look like such a fool? What did I ever do
to this guy?"

"Tate, the guy is crazy. You can't even try
to figure out what his motive is, or why he is,
what he is. He's just crazy and that's all
there is to it."

"It's getting to me and it's getting to me in

a big way."

"Tate, you need to take a few days off. Go up to the cabin and do some fishing. Smoke a few cigars and try to relax. No one knows about the cabin and you will be safe there. Just go and relax and forget about everything."

"You know, I think I'll do it, yes, I'll go up there first thing in the morning. You may be right, it can't hurt, that's for sure."

Chapter twenty-six

The cabin is located about five hours from
Wilmington in the foothills of the Blue Ridge
Mountains. Brad's father left it to him a few
years ago, and he goes up about once every
month for a day or two just to make sure
everything is okay. It's way off the road up a
little winding path that sits just over a
running brook. It is so nice there, especially
in the summertime. It's something about the
cool mountain air and the quietness. The
peace and solitude are calming. It's just what
Tate needs. He's driving up the road toward
the cabin on a rental car that one of the police
officers rented for him. They were very
careful getting the car to Tate, because of the
crazy man that has been taunting him.
On arrival, Tate parked next to the front door
and grabs his bag, fishing rods, and three
cigars and walked in the front door. *Man, it*

feels good to get here, Tate's thinking as he puts his bags and rods down. The rustic atmosphere and the solitude are just right. And, Tate's about to take a noonday nap. But not until after he smokes one of those cigars while sitting in the swing on the front porch. *Man, this place is so relaxing,* Tate thinks as he swings slowly in the cool mountain air. After the cigar, he walks into the cabin to the bedroom. He slips his shoes off, loosens his shirt collar, and lays across the big bed. In a few minutes, Tate's sawing those proverbial logs. He's out, like a light and he'll be out for about three hours. Suddenly, Tate's awakened by a gunshot off in the distance. Then, another and another. Tate jumped up and scrambled to his feet. Who the heck is up here shooting? Hunting season is not in and there should be no one around for miles. So, who's shooting? The shooting stopped as suddenly as it started. But who, and why was there someone shooting? Tate slipped his shoes on and walked out to the back to try and see if he could find out who was shooting. He stands

still and listens intently, but he hears nothing.
Everything is back to normal. So, after a
while, Tate goes back into the cabin. He's
getting a little hungry, so he goes out to his
rental car and gets a large cooler that he
packed for the trip. Some fresh bacon and
eggs with a hot pot of coffee would be good.
After going back in and doing a little
cooking, Tate has the mountainside smelling
good. Now he's eating and he's really
relaxing just like Brad told him. *Man, I wish
I had done this sooner,* Tate is thinking as he
finished his food and lights up a cigar.
No phone up here, no need for a phone, even
if he had one it wouldn't work. No signal in
these hills and why would anyone even need
a phone anyway. No pressure, no worries
and no problems.
The sun will be going down in a little bit and
Tate's ready for a good night's sleep. But
old habits die hard, and Tate just can't help
it. He knows he shouldn't do it but, he does
it anyway. He has a large folder of files on
the Williamston case in the car and he's
getting them out. Tate wants to study over

them to see if he can find something that he may have missed.

The kitchen table is a good place to study over these files. So, here he goes… doing what he was not going to do. This was to be a get-a-way, not a work like heck on the Williamston case. But Tate's obsessed over this case and he's going to do what he does. As the sun comes up Tate is fast asleep. He is face down in the middle of all those files on the kitchen table. Well, so much for that good night's sleep and so much for getting away from the office and the case. As Tate wakes up and stretches, he thinks, *what happened? Where did the night go? What's wrong with me? Why can't I let this thing go?*

It's time for a little fishing, just after some more coffee and a little homemade pork sausage, grits, fresh bread, and a big slice of tomato. Tate's got that smell going all over the mountain again. After a big breakfast, Tate grabs his fishing pole and heads down to the creek to do a little fishing. The creek is just a short walk from the back door of the cabin, no more than twenty feet or so. But the good fishing is up the creek a few hundred yards or so.

Tate slowly makes his way up the creek. He's heading in the direction of where those shots came from. But Tate's not thinking about that, he's only thinking about the fish he wants to eat for dinner and the fun that he will have catching them.

Finally, he's at that big belly of water in the creek that has been known to hold those humongous trout. First cast, and he's got a nice one on the line.

"Man! He's a big one…!" Tate said as he reals him in. Tate's having the time of his life. Tate's too busy to see that strange looking man standing over behind him. The man stood very still and quiet, as he gave Tate the once-over. He's a white male, about 6'3" 250lb dark complexion, wearing old dirty coveralls with heavy blood stains on the right upper front leg. The old dirty straw hat that sat high on his shaggy head, was about done for. His full beard was as black as coal…all except the dark brown tobacco stain that ran down his chin. No shirt and a big belly to go with everything else, said that this man was one that did not see many people from town, or anywhere else as far as that goes. Oh, and he did have in his right hand a very large double barrel shotgun. Tate got that fish and he is getting the hook from his mouth. Now as he turns to get his fish basket, Tate can see the mountain man with his peripheral vision. It startles Tate, to say the least.

"Hello! How are you doing today?" Tate asked.

"I'm doing okay, and you?"

"I'm doing good now...the fish are biting."

"Where did you come from?" The man asked.

"I'm a city slicker that just needs a little time off." Tate's very uneasy, especially with the big mountain man and his long shotgun that's pointed in his direction.

"I heard some shots yesterday, by chance, was that you?"

"Yeah, I shot me a deer...been hunting for a week and had not seen anything till that

thing walked by. Sure was glad to get'em.
The fish are good, but a little meat is nice
once and a while."

"Look, partner, you're making me nervous
with that shotgun pointing in my direction.
Could you point that thing away from my
direction?"

"Sure thing, friend." As he slowly puts the
gun on a large rock next to where he was
standing.
Tate's feeling a little better now, but he's still
unsure about this guy.

"Sir, would you like to do a little fishing? I
have another rod if you would like to join
me?"

"No…no thank you I'll just be moving on
now." The man slowly said as he turned to
walk away.

"Sir! You forgot your shotgun!"

"Thank you." The man said as he turned
and picked the gun up to leave.
As he walked into the woods, he stopped at a
spring, picked a dipper up from a large flat
rock and had him a cool drink of water. As
Tate looked on, he thought that a cool drink

would be nice. So, he walked over to the fellow and asked if he could have a drink.

"Sure… go on and have a drink, but whatever you do, don't mess with this spring. It's where most people around here get their water and it's as clean as can be." After a minute or so the mountain man got up and walked off into the woods and disappeared. Tate couldn't help but think about this strange fellow. Would he return and try something with that shotgun? Or was he harmless?

Tate's back to fishing and he's doing very well. He's catching fish one after another. He soon has more than he can eat. So, he heads back to the cabin and prepares the fish to be cooked. The day goes by fast and Tate has his dinner on the table; freshly fried trout, home fried potatoes with onions, hushpuppies, coleslaw and sweet tea. It just does not get any better than this. After dinner, Tate's mind goes straight back to Williamston and all those murder cases. He just can't get it off his mind. However, he feels very safe from any kind of threats that would have been coming his way back in town. After his meal, Tate heads to the bedroom for a little nap. He's almost asleep as soon as his head hits the pillow. But it's not a sound sleep. He's having very bad dreams of that Thin Man and what he's been doing to everyone. He can't get Williamston off his mind even in his sleep. At least, he's safe up here. 'Or is he?' After all, the wild looking mountain man may slip back up and pull something. The only thing Tate needs to hear now is the banjo picking.

Chapter twenty-seven

"No!! No!!" Tate yells as he jumps up from his bed. Tate was having another very bad dream. The t-shirt he has on is so sweaty that it's sticking to him like duct-tape. Tate sits on the side of the bed holding his head, rubbing his eyes. He slowly gets up and walks to the bathroom and runs cold water onto his face. After a few minutes, he's back into all those files. But he's still not getting anywhere. Is it going to be another night like last night? He's thinking. *No! I can't do it!* He is thinking that he should not have come up here. It was nice of Brad, but this is not working out at all. Now he wants to go back home, but it's too late and he will have to spend another night here. He does, at least, pack all those files and take them back to his vehicle.

No phone, no TV, not even a radio. No

wonder these people look like that man I saw today. No wonder they are crazy. But I've got to stay till morning and I just might as well make the best of it. Tate reaches for one of Brad's books on a shelf in the living room. It's, *To Kill a Mockingbird*, one of Tate's favorites. They say the book is much better than the movie. It's a classic and Tate will have it all read before midnight. As Tate puts the book on the floor next to the bed, he turns out the light and rolls over to try and get some sleep. Within ten minutes, Tate's fast asleep and this time, no dreams. The rest of the night is uneventful and very quiet. Morning is coming fast. The sun is trying to come over the hill and a glimmer of light begins to flash through the window.

Tate is beginning to wake up and he can smell coffee brewing. Hmmm, this is strange because, there is no automatic coffee pot in the cabin and Tate is not brewing coffee.

"What? What's going on here?" Tate said, as he stumbled from the bed and headed to the kitchen. In a flash, Tate's in the kitchen and he could see the coffee maker perking coffee, but there was no one in the cabin but him. Someone has been here and now Tate is in a frenzy. Has Brad come up, made the coffee and left without saying anything? Who? And where are they now? Was it that strange mountain man or someone like him? Now, Tate quickly puts his clothes on and runs out to the driveway to check for extra tire tracks. No other tracks, his car tracks are the only ones in the dirt driveway. Now, this is a mystery! Who in the heck was quiet enough to enter the cabin, make the coffee and leave without making a sound? Well, there is one thing for sure, Tate's not having coffee or anything else here today.

Tate's in a real panic. He's got to get out of the cabin. He's got to do it quickly. First, he has got to do a few things to the cabin that Brad asked him to do. He's got to unplug things, cut the hot water heater off and clean up as best he can. Making up the bed with fresh sheets was not something that he really wanted to do, but he hurriedly took care of things. He quickly finishes and he's ready to head back out to his car to leave this place. Now, Tate's walking out the door, but he was not ready for what was about to happen to him. Much to his shock and dismay, he heard a pump shotgun rachet a round into the chamber, from behind him. It's a sound that brings fear into the heart of anyone on the receiving end. Oh no, Tate thinks. Could this crazy mountain man have just slipped up on me, and now he's planning to make a move? Then, that voice behind him...the voice that he fears and hates with a passion.

"Ha Ha Ha Ha Ha! Tate! Get your hands up and slowly turn around!"
A cold chill run over Tate's body as he slowly turns toward Williamston.

"Mr. Williamston..." Tate said as he looks into Williamston's cold blue eyes. Yes, there he stands, only this time he's not looking like any of his alter egos. He's playing the part of Williamston. No makeup or clown suits or masks of any kind.

"How did you guess? Ha Ha Ha Ha!!" Williamston said with a cool and confident voice.

"How did you find me?! You demented pervert!!"

"You know you can't elude the inevitable! I knew you would be needing to get away for a while. I figured that you would be driving a rental car. I also knew that you would try to hide someplace away from the public. Just a simple tax records check on some of your best friends…Brad! There it was, this nice little mountain cabin that his father gave him. Oh…It almost worked. I drove up early this morning, parked down the road and walked up around the side of the creek and right by that nice spring. That water was extremely and completely refreshing! Ha ha ha ha. But I would not want any of it now! Ha ha ha!"

"You're a sick, sick man and you need help! You really need to see a psychiatrist! You will not get away with this!"

"Oh boy, Suggs was right about you. You are a very heavy sleeper. When I looked in the bedroom window this morning, you were snoring like a freight train. You know that coffee that I made while you were sound asleep was just the icing on the cake for me.

Ha ha ha ha!"

As he said that he takes Tate's service pistol and ordered him back into the cabin.

"So unfortunate for you...have a seat, Tate. We're going to finish playing the game."

"Sure, we are! You psychopath, you love playing these games, don't you!"

"Now you're just mad because you can't ever win. Don't exacerbate, just relinquish and surrender. Ha ha ha! You know how deliriously thoughtful, relentless and cautious I am." Williamston hands Tate a pair of handcuffs and orders him to put them on behind his back.

"And you had better apply them in the proper manner, good and tight!"

"You know you are not going to kill me. If you do, this stupid game, would be over and then what would you have to do? Or who would you have to torment?"

"The game is almost over Mr. Logan and you have lost every time. You're a very poor loser. You're oblivious, moronic, and you're also no good at this game. You've been so easy. You are no fun anymore!"

Tate's in a real mess. He has that helpless feeling and as he tries to think of what to say, he spots movement outside the cabin. *Could it be Brad and the team coming to rescue me?* he thinks.

"Williamston, you know this was a set up to catch you! The Captain and a team of highly trained police officers are here, and they will kill you!"

"Now Tate…do you really think that will work on me? We both know there's not a living soul around here for miles."

"Give it up! You know they are out there!"

"Ha Ha Ha Ha!! Tate, I'm going to kill you and there's absolutely nothing you can do, and you know it! Tate… now, Tate…how diaphanous you are. But as despondency falls over you, the despicable is so desideratum."

"Cut the gobbledygook!! You are so, supercilious!! You're not getting by with anything! My friends are going to get your sorry behind!"

Williamston slowly walked back to the front porch and picked up a small black doctor's bag, that was sitting next to the doorway. He then walked back into the kitchen and over to the kitchen table. He places the bag on the table, opens it up and slowly removes an ice pick, a pair of pruning shears and some rubber gloves. After placing the items on the table, he pulls a straight back chair over in front of Tate and sets the chair about three feet from Tate. Now, he sits directly in front of Tate. "Okay, Tate I will try to talk on a third-grade level. That's the only way you will understand me when I communicate with you. Tate look into my eyes… he said with a very sad look on his face. What do you see Tate?"

"I am looking into the eyes of a very deranged person, and to be honest, I really hate you!"

"But Tate, as I think back to the day my dear old Grandfather picked me up from that hospital, memories begin to flood my mind. Tate… can I tell you my thoughts?"

"Sure…whatever, I don't have anything else to do." Tate said sarcastically.

"Tate, other than my Grandfather, you are

the only real friend that I've ever had…as strange as that may sound."
Now as if he's in a trance of some kind, Williamston starts telling Tate all about his life after he went to live with his grandfather.

"Life with my dear old Papa…that's what I always called him… He was a very good man, unlike my father. He was also, very well to do and very private. I had never seen him, and no one ever talked about him. It seems that he and my father had some type of falling out before I was born. Papa told me once that he loved my father, but they just did not get along. Papa was also a tall man; he was about your size and weight. He liked to wear the very best clothes and he kept himself looking very neat and clean. He had a thick mustache and loved to smoke a pipe. And he cursed like no one I have ever heard before. In his later years, he used a walking cane. He had a very loud and somewhat gruff voice. But I sure loved that man. He was, in his way, very good to me.

"I found out from one of my caretaker's years after Papa died, that the reason father and Papa did not get along, was because of my mother. Yes, it happened that Papa did not want my father to marry her. He knew how she was, and he tried to tell father, but he would not have it. So, he married her and cut off all connections with Papa…" Now, a long pause from Williamston, while Tate looked on.

"…Papa had a few people that worked for him and they all had to sign a confidentiality disclosure agreement. They lived in Papa's big house and only one person could travel to town and back. This was to get supplies and food. The big old house was in the southern part of Virginia, near the North Carolina line. It sat on about five hundred acres deep in the woods. If anyone ever needed a doctor, Papa would call an old fellow that he knew to come and treat them. If they got sick enough to go to the hospital, he would take care of them but, they were never allowed to return.

"Now, this was a very strange situation, but it all worked well for Papa. As for my education, he would have some of the smartest people around to come into the house to school me 'one on one.' You could say that I was given the best of the best. Yes, I had a very good education, one that most people would not have received even at some of the most prestigious and acclaimed schools in the country." Williamston said as though he's still in a trance.

"Papa was only sixty years old when he got me, but most people thought he was in his eighties. He liked looking older for some reason. But there was one thing that he never liked, and I really don't know why. It was his name, Reginal Albert Williamston. He hated that name, and he never used it, as a matter a fact he changed it. Yes, he changed it... of all names... why he picked this I will never know. But he would be called by everyone that knew him, as, Sir William.

"Only a very few people even knew him. His father had died, and I think you know all about his fate. Papa was very rich, reclusive, and quite lonely. But growing up he was faced with a stigma of being a mass murderer's son. The ridicule and shame he must have endured... I guess... in a way he was trying to protect me from the same kind of punishment…I don't know."

Tate's still sitting and hoping that what he might have seen outside was, in fact, a person that would come in and save him. But for now, he will have to keep Williamston talking. Every minute is like gold.

"Wait…wait a minute… if dear old Papa hated his name so much…why in the world did he name his son after himself?"

"I also had a problem with that. It seems that Papa had to name my father after himself due to some crazy loophole in his crazy father's will. For some reason, my great grandfather wanted his son and his grandson and so on, to have that name." Williamston said.

"You know, I remember the day that the town bully beat up Papa's man that used to go into town. The poor man got back home and fell out of the old truck in the driveway. He was as bloody as could be. It took him a few weeks before he was able to get around and he never did get back to normal. But one

thing for sure, that bully would never mess
with anyone from Papa's place ever again.
Yes, it seems that he was invited out to meet
with me and Papa. We met at the big gate to
Papa's place one day. I was only fifteen at
the time, but I will never forget that day.
When the guy drove up and got out of his old
car, he started cursing Papa and me. Papa
just started to laugh at'em, and the more Papa
laughed, the angrier that bully got. Then for
no reason at all, he ran at Papa…big
mistake!" Now, another long pause from
Williamston before he starts back up again.

"It all happened so fast…I remember
stepping in front of Papa and flipping the guy
over my back onto the pavement. He got up
and came at me again, and he hit the
pavement once more. For some reason he
pulled a pocketknife from his pocket and
came at me once more. I remember that
sound…the sound of his right arm breaking,
and that loud yell he let out when he hit the
pavement once more. It was the first time
that I ever inflicted so much pain on anyone.
Yes! Just for the fun of it, I broke his left

arm and several of his ribs. As Papa was still laughing, the bully somehow got into his old car and with 'a hell of a lot of pain' and blood everywhere. He drove away… Ha ha ha ha!!"

The expression on Williamston's face changed once more. The smile left his face, but the blank look in his eyes lingered on as he said;

"Even with all that, I still felt trapped in that big house. Sure, I had it made, and I was getting the best education that money could buy, but I was missing out on life. The only girl that I ever saw from the time I was nine till the time I turned sixteen was one that somehow got onto our grounds. I only saw her from the window as one of Papa's employees escorted her off the property. You see we did not even have a television in that big house. Life was much different for me and sometimes I just think about how it could have been if I would have only had a normal upbringing." For a while Williamston just sits there with a somewhat blank look on his face. And, Tate…well he was still as quiet as a mouse.

Now, Williamston begins to speak:

"When I turned twenty years old, Papa suddenly died. And it was a mess…his caretakers called the ambulance and his attorney. As his body was taken away, the attorney met me at the door. He told me that my life would change and change in a big way. At the time, I had no idea just how much my life would change. I was so rich and so immature. Why, I did not even have a driver's license. As a matter a fact, I had never even driven a car. So, I had to start learning all the things, that most everyone else took for granted. But even with all the money and education, I would be lost in the real world. Slowly I started getting out some…one of Papa's caretakers wanted to help me. The first time we went out, we went to a bar. To make it a little easier on me, we went into the bar at about five in the afternoon. There was almost no one in there, but it was still a shock to me. I drank a beer, and with just one, I got high."

Williamston stops for a minute and starts to

smile. "It took several times for me to get where I felt comfortable…and the beer got better and better, and we went later and later. No one realized just how much money I had, which was good. It kept me from having to deal with a bunch of users and fake friends. Then, one night she came up to me…she was the most beautiful thing that I had ever seen. I felt emotions that I had never felt, but I was such a fool. She had a body that was like a model and a face that was like an angel. She had long black hair that went down to her butt, smooth dark skin, big brown sexy eyes, and she had a set of very big… well, you know.

"She got to me…and man…did she get to me… I was in love. The caretaker tried to tell me to be careful, but no, no…I would not hear him. Just after about a week, I asked her to marry me and she said yes. She wanted a big wedding, but I put my foot down, and we had a very small wedding and a very short honeymoon. We went to Las Vegas, and was I ever lost, but she really knew her way around. It was there that I began to see just who she was...I had made a big mistake! But I loved her more than life." Now, Williamston gets this blank look on his face once more.

"She seemed to change. Slowly and surely, she was turning into my mother. She would go out and sometimes she would not come back home for two or three days. I had no idea where she was. It was driving me crazy. I never wanted to leave the house, I just did not like the outside, but she was always gone.

"Shortly after we were married, I found Mr. Suggs in a jail cell. I had one of my attorneys get him out of jail, and I set'em up in the little old house behind the big old house, that had belonged to Father. For some reason, I had him keep mother and father's bedroom clean and neat. I would check on him from time to time, and I kept him up and looked after'em. But I was having a really hard time with my wife. I made myself happy for almost ten years. I would often go see Mr. Suggs and I even taught him to cook. The food he prepared was the best. He was like the best friend that I ever had. And I knew that his twin brother was my mother's lover. But Suggs was not like his brother at all.

"Yes…I put up with my wife for ten years. She did her thing and I did mine, then one day I found out just how bad she was. I had a private investigator follow her for two weeks. When he gave me a report along with a video tape. It sickened me to the core. That witch was just like my evil mother. She was having sex with several different men. It was devastating to me.

"So… I, like my father, set out to teach her a lesson. I really did not want to kill her. I just wanted to teach her a lesson. But things got out of hand and I did it…I killed her. I made her suffer and before she died, she was begging me to just kill her, and get it over with. It was very bad for her, but not so bad for me.

"It was at that point that I changed, and I really changed. I was no longer the good and unassuming, honest and faithful friend. I had just become my father and my great grandfather, but I was determined to be much better at murder than they were. You see, they did not understand how to play the game at all. No, they were a pair of dumb buttholes for sure. Really! Who kills someone then turns around and kills themselves? No...no it just doesn't work that way!"

At this point, Williamston's expression changed, from a blank look to an angry and anguished look. Then, once more with his eyes wide open, as if he is seeing nothing, and no telling what is going on in his mind, he continued;

"Yes, I would kill again and again and again, and you know what? It felt good! It felt so good to kill someone, and I could not, and would not, and will not stop killing people! I started being a loner... but to hide, I did it right in the open. Somehow, I joined up with the carnival. It was there that I expanded my knowledge of the art of disguise. An old man that had been hooked up with the carnival for many years, taught me everything he knew. And he was very good. But I was much better in the end than he was.

"Oh… and before I forget! That Not Guilty that was handed down in Tony's murder…let's just say… the Foreman of the Jury…well, he's a lot richer today! Ha ha ha ha! The things people will do for a little money."

He just dropped his head and said;

"Now Tate, I have got to kill you, and you are the best friend that I've had in many years."

Tate is thinking; *Why, has he told me all this?'*

"Tate, you know what these are for…don't you?" As he points toward the items on the table. Tate's sitting in the straight back chair in the middle of the floor. Williamston is now standing between him and the front door to the cabin, which is currently standing open. Now, Tate knows that he is going to have to put up a fight. But with his hands cuffed behind him, as he sits in that chair, he knows it will be hard. The fear on Tate's face is very clear to Williamston. It's a sight that he's seen so many times in the past ten years.

Williamston slowly brings the ice pick up and moves closer to Tate.

"Tate, can you hear me?" Hahahaha!"

"Yes! I can hear you! You, crazy fool! You are not going to get by with this!" Williamston comes very close and puts the pick within an inch of Tate's left ear and said;

"Tate, it will be quick…very quick! I have tried and tried, but the recidivism just keeps me coming back! So, now I will try to be a little more phlegmatic…just for you. Ha ha ha ha!" Tate's horrified and at his wit's end. He thinks. *How could I have let this crazy man get the best of me? Is this the end. Who did I see outside the cabin? Will someone come in and stop this nut before it's too late?* Suddenly, Williamston stepped back and started that crazy laugh again.

"Ha ha ha ha ha! Tate, I just want to say…I really hate to kill you! But it's got to be done! And I will admit, you sure come close to getting me…Yes, you did! You got so close, but you just could not do it, could you?" Williamston would inch closer and closer to Tate, with that ice pick and a crazy look on his face. What could be causing him to act this way? Was he having second thoughts or was he just tormenting Tate? Tate said:

"I have two questions?"

"Okay Tate, what's on your feeble little mind?"

"Why did you kill Suggs? He looked after you, and he did everything you asked of him, for all those years. Why!? And, how did you change from one disguise to another so fast? One minute you were Waters and the next minute you were Suggs…"

"Tate, he was of no more use to me, and he had become too close to you, so that's why! He was my servant! Not yours! And as for me being able to change so fast… You know, you have asked me that before and at the time I would not tell you. But now…I'll tell you! Let's just say… I am 'The Master of Disguise and you are The Mark!' Stop, stalling for time! Your time has expired! Fatalism! Ha Ha Ha Ha." Williamston said.

Tate frantically said;

"Look, I've got to asked you one last question!"

"Tate...stop stalling!"

"Did you save one of your wife's fingers!?"

"Oh yes, Tate. She was my first and I did keep her right pinky. And she knew it too."

"What did you do with her body?"

"I cut her up into little pieces and put them into a big barrel of caustic acid, that was in an old building on Papa's property. Now, there is no more of her, and there will never be any more of her! Ha ha ha ha! To Be, or Not, To Be! Is that the question!? That's the last question, Tate! This is the end!" As Williamston draws back to kill Tate.
Now, Tate readies himself for unwelcomed death...how a moment in time can seem so quick, but, yet so slow as well. But he's ready and he believes that when he passes over that he will be with God. You see Tate is a believer and has been one from the time he was a little boy.

Chapter twenty-eight

BOOOM!!!

A shotgun blast from the front door rang out! Williamston falls on top of Tate and they both hit the floor. Blood is oozing from Williamston onto Tate. What just happened? Williamston's dead and he's lying on top of Tate. Tate struggled with great confusion to get Williamston off him, but with his hands cuffed and Williamston laying on top of him, he's not doing too well. Suddenly someone pulls Williamston over to one side. As this happens, Tate can see that it's the mountain man. He has just saved Tate's life by shooting Williamston in the back with his shotgun.

"Thank you! Thank you! He was just about to kill me with that ice pick. Why did you shoot him?"

"That son of a gun crapped into our spring

and that's one thing that you just don't do!!!"

"You mean you shot him because he defecated into the spring?"

"No! I shot him because he took a dump in the spring! I also thought you might want me to stop him from sticking that ice pick in your ear."

"Well, how ironic, the pile of poop that I thought would put him on death row, ended up putting him to death. No good investigative work needed here, just good old 'mountain justice,' …yes sir." Tate said as he directed the mountain man to get the keys to the handcuffs off the table.

"Help get these cuffs off me." As the handcuffs are being removed from his wrists.

"Ha Ha Ha Ha Ha!!!" Tate is laughing like crazy, and the mountain man is standing there with a look of surprise.

"What's the matter with you? Mister, why are you going on like this?"

"Ha Ha Ha Ha Ha!! If you only knew! You have just done what no one else could have ever done! We have been trying to get this nut for a long time! And you just got him! He has murdered almost a hundred people in the last ten years and has managed to get completely away with it! Now he's dead and all because he pooped in the spring! Yes, there is justice… Mountain Justice." Tate said, as he looked at Williamston's body lying dead on the cabin floor.

Chapter twenty-nine

Now, Tate is facing a long and hard battle with the FBI. Also, things will be very challenging with several local police departments up and down the east coast. It's a battle that he knows he will lose, now that Williamston's dead. He truly felt that if he could have won the game with Williamston, he would have told the truth about everything that he had done. Then, all those poor people sitting in prison could have been turned loose. But now, with Williamston dead, it will be impossible, and Tate will have to live with this the rest of his life. Even with the death of Williamston, Tate still lost the stupid game.

"I need to drive back down the mountain so that I can call the police to come up here and investigate this. You will need to go with me. Just leave the shotgun on the floor next to Williamston. We can lock the cabin door and with some rope in the old tool barn, we can cordon off the scene. Don't worry you are not in any trouble. How could you be? You saved my life. You are a hero." Tate said as he pulled his cell phone from his bag that was sitting on the front porch. After driving down the mountain and calling 911 to report the incident to the local Sheriff, Tate heads back to the cabin to meet the officers that will be investigating the incident. Tate and the mountain man arrive about five minutes before the officers do. As Tate and the mountain man sit in Tate's vehicle, the officers pull into the yard, park and get out to meet Tate and the mountain man near the front door to the cabin.

"Are you Detective Logan?"

"Yes, I am."

"Can you tell us what happened here?" Tate tells the officer everything that has happened, and it takes a few minutes to do so. Then, they take the officers into the cabin where Williamston was.

"Man…he's dead alright…" The officer

said as he made a note on his notepad. The overweight, short, red-faced, big nosed, long-haired middle-aged officer said,

"Officer, do you have a CSI unit in your department?"

"Yes. I guess that would be me…you see we don't really have CSI up here."

"I know that I am out of my jurisdiction, but I think we need to get the State to come in to assist you on this, due to the nature of the case."

"No. The Sheriff will not be calling those guys. He's had some problems with them in the past and he's not going to call."

"Look, officer, the FBI has been looking into this guy. I would like to call them in to help out."

"Mister! If you want to make the Sheriff mad, you call the SBI or the FBI and you're in a lot of trouble!"

Tate's in a mess, and he can see big trouble coming if the Feds are not called and called very soon.

"Officer, it's not that I don't trust you, it's just that this man on the floor has killed a hundred people in the last ten years."

"I don't care about that. Now, if you want to ask the Sheriff, go for it. I know what he's going to say. And that is, NO!"

"Okay, whatever you say, I understand. I have one question."

"Sure, and what's the question?"

"Can I take a few pictures of the body?"

"Sure, but I am in control here and not you. You need to understand that. If so, we will not have any problems."

So, Tate starts taking pictures of Williamston with his cell phone. While the Deputy goes back out to his vehicle for another pen. Tate quickly goes into Williamston's pockets. He removes Williamston's wallet, and some papers before the officer can get back inside. He can hear the officers coming back onto the front porch. Tate quickly hides the wallet and the papers as the officer comes into the room. Tate's back to taking pictures, as the officer comes into the room. The Officer tells Tate;

"You have to stop taking pictures and leave the area."

"Yes Sir, Officer, whatever you say." Tate walks out of the cabin.

On the way to his car, Tate can see one of the officers questioning the mountain man. He can hear the mountain man tell the officer that his name is Tyson Laney and that he lives about two miles up the mountain in the family cabin. It has no address and never has had one. Tate places his bag into his car and starts to leave the area. As he's backing out to turn around, the Deputy that was inside came running out yelling for Tate to stop.

"What is it, Officer?"

"You may need to stay around for a while, I might have some more questions for you."

"Officer, I have told you everything that I know and if you need me, you have my phone number, just call me. I have got to go. I am late for a meeting in my town."

"Okay…okay, go on. But don't get any ideas about calling the State or the Feds."

"Okay officer, don't worry, I won't call anyone." Tate said as he quickly backed out of the driveway.

Chapter thirty

As Tate heads down the mountain, he's trying to reach the FBI, but he will not get a signal for at least another three miles.   In about five minutes, he gets Jim with the FBI.

"Jim! This is Tate Logan."

"Yes, Tate what can I do for you?"

"Jim, he's dead. Williamston is dead."

"What did you say? For a moment there I thought you said that Williamston was dead."

"Yes! That's what I said! He's as dead as can be. Trust me, he's dead."

"Where are you? We need to get there ASAP."

"Jim, he was about to kill me, when an old mountain man shot him in the back! Look, it's a long story. Just get to a town in the mountains of North Carolina. It's called Black Mountain. I can meet you at the Red Roof Inn on Big Hill Drive. I'll get a room, but I will not be using my real name. I will be Archie Bunker. Just hurry up and get here."

"I can get there but, it will be late tonight."

"That's okay, just get here ASAP. These local-yocals are going to mess this thing up if you don't get here soon."

"Yeah, Tate they always give us a hard time. But don't worry, we'll get them straight." After talking with Jim, Tate calls Brad:

"Brad, Williamston is dead…he was killed inside your cabin. I'm sorry for the mess, but I will clean everything up."
Then Brad said;

"What did you just say? For a minute, I thought you said, Williamston was dead."

"Yes Brad, he's dead…he was about an inch from killing me when an old mountain man shot him in the back and killed'em."

"Are you okay? And, don't worry about the cabin."

"I'm okay, but I've got to meet with Jim from the FBI, and it may be a few more days before I get back to the office."

"Take your time…and I'm glad this nightmare is over."

"Me too Brad and I will fill you in as soon as I can."

It's about midday and Tate has checked into room 304 at the Red Roof Inn. He has tried to hide his vehicle at the rear of the motel so that the tag number cannot be seen. After getting settled in, Tate pulls out that wallet and paper that he removed from Williamston. There is not much in the wallet, just some ID cards that have AKA names and addresses. There is also about seven thousand dollars in cash. One of the paper notes has a suspicious message on it. It says; 'One and One + 2 = 1 - 87-12-91, will get you close to me. Find the hidden message and you will find the treasure.' On the back of the paper were the words:

"Looks like you have won! But you still have work to do, to get the prize."

Tate knows that this message is for his eyes and his eyes only. It's Williamston's way of dragging this game out, even though he's dead. Tate's sick to his soul about this, but there is nothing he can do. He may never solve this puzzle and even if he does, what would the outcome be?

Tate's been in the room for several hours and he's trying to understand what the crazy message means, but he's not having any luck. Now, the phone in his room rings.

"Call for Mr. Bunker." The lobby receptionist said.

"Okay, thank you operator."

Then Jim comes on the line,

"I'm in the lobby."

"Come on up, the door will be open." Tate responded.

About three minutes later, Jim came into the room.

"Okay Tate, what the heck's going on?"

Tate goes through what had taken place over the last few days. Then, he shows Jim the suspicious note that Williamston left Tate.

"Jim...what the heck does this mean? I have tried and tried to understand what he's telling me but it's not making any sense."

"Tate, one + one + 2 = 1. Why Tate he's talking about himself. Remember, those different personalities totaled four, it really was only one. He's saying that he's the one. And now the numbers appear to be the combination to a safe. What else would a treasure be stored in?"

"So where would that safe be? That's the question."

"I know! I know where that safe could be!" Tate yelled out.

"Well, where is it?"

"It's someplace in that old house in Richmond, Va."

"Tate you may be right. We both may be headed into a trap."

"The only way to find out, is to get on up there and see."

"Okay, Tate let's get a good night's sleep and head up first thing in the morning." This will be a long night for Tate and Jim. They have no idea what may lay in store for them at that old house. They may have missed all the clues completely. It just seemed a little too easy to Tate. This guy was much smarter than that. As Tate slept, he has a dream, and in the dream, the Thin

Man is laughing at him and taunting him.
'Tate! You're STUPID! I have beaten you!
I have beat you every time you have turned
the corner! You are so STUPID!
Hahahahah!!'

Chapter thirty-one

Tate's had a long miserable night. It's now time to get up and get ready to meet Jim and head to Richmond. Then as Tate is gathering his belongings and preparing to leave the room, Jim knocks at the door.

"Tate! Are you ready?"

"Yes, Jim I'm ready." Tate said as he walked out the door to meet Jim. They both signed out of the hotel and drove to a nice little restaurant for some breakfast. As they were eating their breakfast, Tate looks up to see the deputy sheriff coming in, and he's headed their way.

"Oh no Jim, here comes that local deputy sheriff, and he's locked in on me."

"Don't worry, Tate, let me take care of him."

"Okay Jim, he's all yours."

"Mr. Logan, you left the area a little too

quickly yesterday. I had a few more questions for you."

"Sorry about that. By the way, let me introduce you to my friend."

"No Tate, let me tell the gentleman who I am and what I'll be doing here today." Jim said with a big smile on his face.
At this time, Jim showed the deputy his badge and said,

"You know, withholding information from a federal agent is 'Obstruction of Justice' and carries very large and heavy criminal judgments. I also understand that the man that was killed yesterday, was being investigated by the FBI and you told this off-duty police officer that 'no one would be calling the FBI. Now is that what happened?"

"No Sir, we were going to call you today. Yes, we were. Thank you for coming to help us with this case." The deputy said, as he nervously wiped the sweat from under his hat.

"Thank you very much Officer, I'm sorry for the misunderstanding. There will be two

Special Agents in your office in the next hour. You don't want to miss seeing them."

"Yes, Sir! Yes, Sir." The deputy turned and nervously walked out the door, as Tate and Jim laughed to themselves.

It was a long drive, but Jim and Tate had arrived at the old Williamston house. Now, where do they start the search?

"Tate, where do you think we need to start?"

"Jim lets go into that bedroom. It's in there someplace... maybe, a hidden wall safe, maybe a floor safe, who knows. I just believe that it's in there somewhere."

"Tate, that's as good a place as any to start, let's go." Jim said as they ducked under the crime scene tape and headed up the front steps.

As they walk into the dirty old house and up the stairs, Tate can't help but remember the first time he walked into the room. He had a real funny feeling and it was not that Ha Ha, type of feeling. Now, they are inside the bedroom. The old bed and that big trunk at the foot of the bed are still here. However, the jar of fingers and the clown suits have been removed. They both just stand there looking all around the room. They both look at the very large painting at the head of the bed. "This would be a good place for a wall safe." Jim said. As Tate walks to the right side of the head of the bed, he looks down, and he can see some scuff marks on the floor.

"What could have caused these scuff marks?" Tate asked.

"They line up with the bottom of that large bedpost."

"Yes, it looks like someone has been moving the bed around so as to get behind the bed."

"Tate, you are right, let's move the bed to see what's behind that large painting. I wonder who that man is in that old painting?"

"It's more than likely Williamston's father. It resembles Williamston." Tate said.
Jim got down on the floor and looked under the bed. As he looked under the bed, he could see a metal lever, that was hooked to a large wheel. He pressed the lever down and

the wheel pushed down on the floor. The bottom of the bed moved upward. It appeared to be designed to let the bed roll around from the wall.

He stood up and said;

"Tate help me push the bed around at the bottom." The two moved the bed with ease, although the top right bedpost did touch the floor, just enough to mark the floor. Once the bed was away from the wall, the two walked up to the painting. It looks like the painting is somehow mounted to the wall. Tate and Jim are wondering why it would be mounted so secure and not just hung. After a few minutes and not getting any place with the painting, Tate walks over to a bookcase on the same wall to the left of the bed. There are several books and some very pricey antiques sitting in the bookcase. Jim walked over and started looking at the items.

"Look, Jim do you see all the dust on these things?"

"Yes, I do… all but the funny looking paperweight near the end."

"Yes, I saw that. Now, look what happens

when I move it."

As Tate moved it, the large painting started to come away from the wall.

"Look! You did it! You've done it!" Jim yelled.

Tate ran over to the painting and there it was, a very large wall safe.

"We found it! We found it!" Tate yelled.

"Open the thing man!" Jim said.

"I can't do it. I just can't do it. My nerves are shot and who knows... the thing may be booby-trapped."

"Tate, you're right, I'm going to call the Bomb Unit, and they can get the safe open." This could be big, extremely big. There could be millions of dollars or a bomb ticking away inside. But whatever's in it will have to wait another hour. About forty-five minutes later the Bomb Unit arrived and sent Tate and Jim out of the room, some 200 yards down the road.

Minutes seemed like hours to Tate. He was so pumped up. What the heck's in that safe? After about twenty minutes, Jim received a call that they had opened the safe. There was a bomb inside the safe, and the Bomb Unit was able to defuse it. But what else was inside that safe?

Jim and Tate went back into the room and the commander of the Bomb Unit told them that they could examine the contents. As they walked over, Jim looked at Tate and said,

"Tate would you please do the honors?"

"Yes Sir! I would love to."

As Tate looked inside, he could see a gold box in the back. It's much bigger than a shoe box.

"It's okay Tate, the Bomb Unit has cleared it too." Jim said as Tate reached and pulled the box out.

"Let's see what's in it."

Tate said as he slowly opened the box. Much to their surprise, the box was full of small VHS tapes and each one was marked and dated. Each one had a murder victims name written on it. The very first tape on the very top of the stack was addressed to Tate, and it also had the words written in red...

"View this tape first. and the envelope last!"

In the very bottom of the box, was an

envelope that looked like a legal document, that was also addressed to Tate.

"What in the world could this be?" Tate said.

"It could be related to all those murders. Who knows?"

"It very well could be. The only way to find out is to look at every one." Tate said with a big smile.

"Jim, even after he's dead, he's still controlling me. He wants me to look at this tape first, and you know…that's what I'm going to do."

They left the area, headed back to the FBI office in Richmond VA.

Chapter thirty-two

Now, at the office, Jim tells Tate to plug the tape in that is addressed to him. So, with some hesitation, Tate slowly plugs it in and hits the play button. Now, there he was, Williamston on tape, looking right into the camera.

"Well, Tate, if you are viewing this tape, that means that you have won the game... Ha Ha Ha Ha!!! But, have you really won, or did you just get lucky! Now Tate, each one of these tapes have all the detail accounts of each murder that I ever committed. Most even have the actual murder on tape. You will even get to see me smash Tony Johnson's head in. You missed that little camera that I had put up on the wall next to the back door at Tony's. Yes, you will see yourself walking all about, just like you think you know it all!

"As for that envelope, please don't open that until after you and your FBI buddy, Jim, have viewed all the evidence on the tapes. Anyway, have fun!!! Ha Ha Ha Ha!!!"
Tate and Jim just look at each other for a minute. Then Tate said;
"Okay, Jim...let's get with it!"
Tate and Jim looked at all the tapes and were astonished at the gory details of the murders that were perpetrated. All that day and into the evening hours, they watched each tape. Williamston worked with amazing precision and accuracy in each case. It was also the most diabolical display of rage and hatred they would ever witness. They hope that someone will be able to take this new evidence to each person's lawyer, so those innocent people could be exonerated. This was one of the biggest things that ever happened to Tate and it's going to make a lot of people very happy. It will also make a lot of people very unhappy.
Justice will prevail, whatever the cost. Tate remembered that the word justice means peace and to have a genuine respect for

people.

Jim spoke interrupting Tate's thoughts;

"Tate, we have a mountain of evidence here."

"No, Jim what we have, is a, '*Mountain of Justice*' and it will hit very hard."

"Okay, Tate are you ready to see what's in the legal papers?" Jim asked.

"Yes. Let's see what this monster has here." As Tate opened the envelope and removed a document.

"Jim! It's Williamston's Last Will and Testament!"

"Well Tate, read it."

Then, as Tate is reading the thing to himself, the strangest look fell on his face.

"Tate! Tate! What does it say?!"

"Jim the crazy fool just left me everything he had in the world…"

"So, this deranged killer left you everything he had?"

"Yes. He has left me a hundred and fifty million dollars and all his property. He admitted that he was crazy and that he had no control over anything he did. He kept going back to his mother and his father and how they abused him as a child. Then, having a wife that ends up like his mother, did not help. He also said that somehow meeting me made him realize just how messed up he was. Now, that I have won the game, he thinks that I should get the prize."

"Tate, if this thing ends up being legal, you will have it made for the rest of your life."

"Jim, I will give it to the family members of each victim and others that have a real need. I will not keep one red cent."

"Tate, I hope the government stays out of this, you know how they can be in these matters."

"Yes, I know and whatever happens, happens. It would only be justice for the money to go where it should…to the families of those poor victims."

Chapter thirty-three

There are many questions in this matter that
will more than likely never come to light.
How could someone as smart and as rich as
Williamston go from a quiet, seemingly good
person to the evil monster that he became?
How could he go for ten or more years and
be so good to Suggs, while staying out of any
trouble? Then, on a minute's notice, turn and
start murdering people for the fun of it.
One thing for sure, Williamston most
certainly and positively did have the
condition known as, 'Narcissistic Personality
Disorder' or NPD. No, the Sad Clown did
not have the NPD as Dr. Whitfield testified
in court. It was Williamston himself. He had
an attitude built on vanity. Somehow, there
is a thin line between self-esteem and NPD.
When he turned thirty, his self-esteem grew
so large that he crossed that line. Deep in his
core, he must have felt insignificant, with no
accomplishments and an unworthy strive for

greatness. With his very large bank account and his IQ, he knew he could play a very dangerous game. That is what people with NPD do. They love to play games, and they love to win. So, he had to prove something, and he was thinking big. He almost won...

As for Williamston having Dissociative Identity Disorder, we may never know for sure. But with Williamston freely talking about what he saw when his father killed his mother and her lover, it's not likely that he had DID. But with what he went through, it's a wonder that he was able to stay cool for so many years.

The bad thing about Williamston...he was like a missing link. No one seemed to know anything about him, other than what he told Tate in the cabin the day the mountain man killed him. His grandfather, who was somewhat a recluse and a loner himself, raised Williamston from age nine to age twenty. No evidence existed to support him having a wife. There were no records of Williamston attending any schools or colleges. Williamston was more than likely telling the truth about how he was educated. Suggs had told Tate, that during the first ten years of the twenty years he knew him, Williamston treated him very good and seemed to be a very normal person. Then he changed and became very, very bad. So, what Williamston told Tate about his wife and how she drove him over the edge, could have very well been true.

The mind of a serial killer, especially one as smart, cunning, calculating and creative as Williamston could be studied for a long time. It is doubtful that anyone could completely explain his life choices. This was a case that even bewildered famous FBI profilers. A team of special agents, and profilers worked on this case for almost a year, and they could not conclude what happened to Williamston. An autopsy was done, and nothing was found in Williamston's brain that would have caused him to do the things he did. He also had a condition known as 'Psychological Trauma.' The cause of this more than likely started when his mother trapped him into playing her sick games with her lover.

Adding what his father did to Williamston, it really drove him to the point of no return. We can look at Williamston, and you can see that he had all six signs of Psychological Trauma:

Shock, denial and disbelief
Aggression
Issues sleeping
Anxiety. (Remember, he was taking Clonazepam for a reason. It also aids in sleeping.)
Dissociation, detachment of emotions
Physical concerns, emotional behavioral experiences

The events of Williamston's childhood were more than enough to cause anyone serious psychological issues. There was another historical event that was suspicious. It seems that Williamston's great-grandfather on his father's side also had a history of murder. He too, like Williamston III was very smart and very rich, only he was a self-made millionaire. It seems that back in the 1920s, he killed five people in five days, and it took three years for someone to find out he did it. All the people that he killed were total strangers. He perpetrated the murders in a manner that made innocent people pay the price. But lucky for them, Williamston, the great grandfather, was caught and he made a full confession. Then, while in a lonely jail cell late one night, he hung himself with a bed sheet.

It was also surmised but not determined for sure that, it could be a DNA trait that worked its way down to Williamston. So, at this point, no one may ever know. But, if a person can be genetically predisposed to things like cancer, obesity, and several other disorders... then why not the desire to murder? There have been several studies done on this matter. Some say no, and some say yes. But with all that said, it would be taboo, to talk about such a thing. So, for now, we just don't know why Williamston did what he did.

Now about that crazy laugh. What was up with that? It turns out that there are three things that could have caused it.

First, there is Pseudo Bulbar Affect, PBA, a brain disorder that is usually caused by a brain injury. Williamston was beaten by his father. However, the results from the autopsy did not show any brain injury.

Some people get an abnormal and significant neurochemical buzz when committing a crime. This may have been what was going on with Williamston.

Then, there is the cannibalism, which caused him to eat the finger of Doris Dooly? He may have eaten even more human parts from his victims. This is something that we may never know. Williamston would not talk about that. It was like, to him at least, that it never happened. He would not, and never did talk about it. He took that with him to the grave. But it is a known fact that cannibalism is also called the laughing sickness. It seems that it does cause people to laugh. It may have been what caused Williamston to let out that laugh. Detective Tate Logan will remember that laugh forever.

Chapter thirty-four

After all he had been through, Tate had some
conflicting thoughts about our great legal
system. Tate knew he was a cop who was
dedicated to doing the right thing. He did, in
fact, take a hard look at the evidence. He
looked at all the evidence, direct evidence,
circumstantial evidence and the evidence that
some people will never talk about, and that's
exculpatory evidence. Exculpatory evidence
can turn a case completely around and free
the suspect.
It made the power-hungry DA very angry
when Tate attempted to bring the exculpatory
evidence forward. He knew that this
evidence would kill the case and make him
look bad in the eyes of the public. The flip
side of that is, it will keep an innocent person
from being wrongfully convicted.
Unfortunately, in today's world, we have
way too many people that will put winning
over the lives of innocent people. Some

would even say, behind closed doors…so what, if they did not commit this crime, they have committed several more that they got away with.

At times, we can clearly see that the system is broken. It doesn't take a rocket scientist to see that some high-level Washington politicians seem to get by with the most serious crimes, while others are hounded for the slightest little infraction. Yes, it is true, that the very legal system that's supposed to be the best in the world, has now been weaponized to go after political foes. No one seems to care at all, unless you happen to be on the receiving end at the time. This type of activity is very bad for everyone, and it should never be permitted to happen. Yes, it seems that whoever is in control at the time will use the DOJ, FBI or even the IRS to go after people that they think are not on their side. It does seem that the corruption starts at the top and works its way down.

Epilogue

It has been three years and today the last innocent person is coming from the Courthouse as a free man. Like the rest, he is a millionaire. The money he and the others received is not from the hundred and fifty million. It is from the government. Yes, each one of the people that had been wrongfully convicted and sent to prison, have now been released and given five million dollars. Although, this will never make up for the precious time they lost, it can make the rest of their lives much better. All that evidence along with the jar of fingers were connected back to Williamston. Tate's in the crowd of family and friends that are gathered to welcome the innocent person to the outside world again. Every person in the crowd is crying tears of joy.

Tate's been at every welcome home gathering from first to last. Although, he is not in the middle of the crowd, he's just an observer from a distance. As a matter a fact, no one in the crowd realizes that he is even there.

Now, for Tate, he's retired and happily married. Yes, he met the most wonderful woman, a blond-haired beauty by the name of 'Della Mae.' They have settled down in a little retirement area near Wilmington, along with his old friend Brad. As for that hundred and fifty million, the government did not take the money and Williamston had no family left to fight over the assets. Williamston and his father were only children and Williamston's mother had no one left on her side of the family. Tate did manage to get most of it to where he wanted it to go; the families of the people that had been killed by Williamston. After that, he started a nonprofit organization to assist other families in the same situation. True to his word, Tate did not take one red cent. He also found Williamston's five-hundred-acre estate with his papa's very large house. Tate and Della Mae have met each of the people that kept the estate running. Tate has set up a fund that will keep each person living well until they pass. The only requirement is, they are to keep living there and looking after the place as long as they can. Tate has gotten to know each person very well. He and Della have been there many times. Tate just could not leave those people holding the bag with nowhere to go. As for the confidentiality agreement, Tate released them from that long ago. But these people, still to this very day, will not tell anyone, a single word about anything that happened during the time they worked under that agreement.

As for Tyson Laney, the mountain man, Tate took good care of him as well. He is living the good life now. He has a big nice mountain home with running water and all the modern comforts. He also has a nice new four-wheel drive pick-up truck that goes over a new road that Tate had dug into the side of the mountain. Tate and Della Mae have become very good friends with Tyson and his wife Ruthie. Tate and Della Mae often visit with them in their mountain home. They really do love to hear them singing, while

316

Tyson picks his Martin guitar on that big front porch. But there's one thing for sure, if you are ever in that part of the country, you better not mess around that Old Spring.

Bert Whitfield
Mountain of Justice